PRIME SUSPECT

He matched the description. He was big and hairy, dressed in dirty work clothes. His woman stepped back into the camper. He asked, "What's it to you?"

"The sheriff wants to talk to you."

"I don't see no sheriff."

"I'm a deputy. My name's Beard."

He advanced on me. "If your sheriff wants to talk to me, let him come and do it."

I stood my ground. "No, sir. That's not the way he wants it."

"Two different things, what he wants and what he gets." He took two steps and swung.

It was a wild and awkward punch, and I thought, slipping it, that I had no need for fancy stuff. I hit him hard with a left and right.

He roared and tried to close in, wanting to grapple. This time I hit him harder, left and right, and he went down.

I started putting on the handcuffs. Too late, I glimpsed the swing of something dark. It hit me, the edge of a frying pan, I learned later.

I learned a lot of things later. . . .

PLAYING CATCH-UP

A. B. Guthrie, Jr.

BANTAM BOOKS

TORONTO · NEW YORK · LONDON · SYDNEY · AUCKLAND

*This low-priced Bantam Book
has been completely reset in a type face
designed for easy reading, and was printed
from new plates. It contains the complete
text of the original hard-cover edition.*
NOT ONE WORD HAS BEEN OMITTED.

PLAYING CATCH-UP

*A Bantam Book / published by arrangement with
Houghton Mifflin Company*

PRINTING HISTORY
Houghton Mifflin edition published September 1985
Bantam edition / December 1987

*Bantam Books are published by Bantam Books, Inc. Its trade-
mark, consisting of the words "Bantam Books" and the por-
trayal of a rooster, is Registered in U.S. Patent and Trademark
Office and in other countries. Marca Registrada. Bantam
Books, Inc., 666 Fifth Avenue, New York, New York 10103.*

PRINTED IN THE UNITED STATES OF AMERICA

O   0 9 8 7 6 5 4 3 2 1

Again to Carol

If anyone finds a resemblance to himself in these pages, fine and dandy, though I can't imagine who it might be.

1

"It's not the rape that distresses me so much," Madame Simone said to me. Her eyes were green, the shade of spring leaves.

"No?"

"She was a professional girl. She knew men. She had been there, if you see what I mean."

I didn't feel easy here in the parlor of what an old-timer, being polite, would have called a sporting house. The room was all right—all right, that is, if you could accept upholstery of blushing pink and pink lampshades, an oversized, gilt-edged mirror on one wall and, beside it, a sideboard with an array of bottles. No girls waited in line. No one tried to hustle me.

"It was still rape," I said. "A violation of person, and that's a serious crime."

"But to kill her! That gets me. Why did he have to do that?"

She was dressed in a summer suit, cream-colored, with flecks of pink in it and might have just prepared for a visitor or for shopping or for a business session. I could see her sitting in a meeting of some board of directors. Not the ordinary madam, I thought, but a madam all the same no matter how she spelled it. The Simone must have been an invention.

Seated in the chair she had assigned me, I said, "God knows why he killed her, but rape and murder sometimes go together." My eyes went to a polished wooden stairway, but no one was coming down it. "Now the victim, this Laura Jane Smitson, tell me about her."

"I've answered the questions once, to a big, dumb deputy who came here before you."

I knew she referred to Halvor Amussen, who was big and brave but heavy-handed and hardly brilliant. I had studied his notes.

"He may have missed something, or you overlooked something. Now about the girl?"

The cradled phone at her side rang, and she answered, "Yes, Mr. —" Her gaze came to me. "I have arranged everything as you wished. See you then. Thank you."

"The girl?" I prompted.

"She worked for the Overthrust Oil Company. A stenographer."

"She didn't live here?"

"Oh, no. I almost never have resident girls. She lived with her parents."

"Any residents here now?"

"No again. I believe you are thinking of the old-fashioned whorehouse. Mine are respectable town girls. Most of them work during the day. I keep a list. We have nothing in common with those old houses."

Nothing, I thought, but the commodity.

The time was midafternoon. Through a window at the side of the room I could see down a slope to the bridge over Muddy Creek. The creek was the dividing line between the two counties. The body of the girl had been found by two youngsters who were playing on the other side of the bridge.

"I have a good list," Madame Simone went on. "The pill has opened opportunities for the working girl. She adds to her income, and the men get what they want. Everyone's satisfied. A first-class arrangement. Right?"

I had never encountered such matter-of-fact cynicism. Instead of answering, I asked, "Did the girl have regular customers? Was she somebody's favorite?"

"That's confidential. I'm a clam."

"I can have you subpoenaed."

She gave me a half-smile. "I doubt you'd want to

do that. All the broken homes, the divorces, wives mad as hornets. Right in your town, too. Think of the ruined reputations."

"What about her immediate bosses? Were they her customers?"

"Clients, we call them. I'll answer that question, and the answer is no."

The telephone rang again. She said into it, "Yes, of course. I'll see. Could you call me back later?"

"You want to find the murderer, don't you?" I said.

"That's a foolish question. Of course I do."

"Then you might help by telling me the names of her clients."

"Doctors have a right to confidential relationships. So do lawyers. I claim my right. What's more, the names wouldn't help you at all. I'm positive of that."

"You're not being cooperative. Don't you care?"

"Why do you think I'm talking to you? Of course I care. You don't know when a person's hurting." She flung out a hand. "So I talk to you. Talk is like a bandage over a sore. This give-and-take hides the wound."

I thought she might be going to cry, but she straightened her face and asked, "Want a drink? On the house?"

The phone rang again. She let it ring.

I said, "No, thanks."

She gestured toward the sideboard and bottles. "I don't sell drinks. I haven't a license. The drinks are complimentary. A client may need something to encourage him in the first place and something to buck him up in the second."

Again that serene cynicism.

"So," I said for lack of something better, "you make the arrangements and provide the house."

"You're learning."

"Another question. Was there any trouble here at the house before she left for home?"

"What makes you think there was?"

"I'm asking."

She nodded slowly. "For reasons—well, because

fights are bad for my reputation—I haven't mentioned it. And your partner, the deputy who was here earlier, didn't ask. Besides, he rubbed me the wrong way. I don't like to tell you about it now."

"It might help."

I sat and waited.

"He was a ruffian."

"Who was?"

"I didn't get his name, not then and really not at all."

"Maybe you'll remember. Go on."

"He was a stranger in dirty clothes and boots, and he was all hair, head and face. Somehow he found his way here. He saw Laura Jane and wanted her. Not just wanted her. Demanded her. You will understand he wasn't our type. Of course Laura wouldn't have him. So he began shouting, yelling his money was as good as any man's and who did we think we were. He grabbed Laura by the arm."

Madame Simone fell silent as if re-living the scene. I didn't nudge her.

"I have a man here at night. You'd call him a bouncer. I got him in, and he yanked the man away, and I called my friend, our county sheriff. He's quick to send me help. So Mugs and the stranger struggled for a while, and finally the man butted Mugs in the belly and hit him on the chin, and that was it."

"It for Mugs."

"Yes. Then the man grabbed Laura Jane again and tried to wrestle her upstairs. Just in time the deputies arrived."

"And arrested him?"

"He wanted to fight, but one of them laid a billy alongside his head, and the other drew a gun. That calmed the man down except for his tongue. He was still swearing and yelling he had his rights."

"Did they get his name?"

"I told you I didn't get it. Nearest I could come was Ford maybe. What with his mouthing off and Mugs groaning and Laura Jane crying in a corner, it was hard to hear. Being sarcastic, I guess, one of the men called him Mister. Anyhow, that's what it sounded like."

"So they took him in?"

"No. They gave him a lecture and threw him out."

"What! No charges?"

"In my business you can't afford trials. The publicity is bad. The sheriff knows that. This is an orderly house."

"I'll get the name from his office."

"I doubt it. The officers will have thrown away whatever notes they took. There won't be any report."

"They'll remember the name."

"If they do, they won't give it to you. The sheriff doesn't like outsiders to nose into his business."

"Rape and murder are everybody's business."

"But a fight in this house isn't. That's strictly for the county."

"You could ask him to give me the name."

"Even then, even if one of the officers remembers it, you'll be turned down. You see, the sheriff prides himself on keeping order in the town and county. He wants it clean, so he says. That includes this house. He won't let you pry."

"Could you identify the man we're talking about?"

"If I had to, I suppose."

"How much longer did Laura Jane stay? After the man had been marched out, I mean?"

"Quite a while. An hour or more. I tried to keep her here, but she was so upset that nothing would do but to go home. It's only across the creek and to the right. About a quarter of a mile."

The phone interrupted us again.

"What time did she leave?"

"About eleven o'clock. Time for the stranger to be long gone." She rose. "Now I've told you all I know. What about that drink?"

I had one with her and said thanks and goodbye.

2

I sat in the car, not switching it on, and thought about Madam Simone and what she had told me. She had given me kind of a lead. It was slim but better than anything Halvor Amussen had turned up, which was nothing. All we really knew was that Laura Jane Smitson, prostitute, had been raped and choked to death eight nights ago.

And Madame Simone? Her language was clean if her business wasn't. And now I thought it wasn't cynicism I had seen in her but earthiness, which, I supposed, was a kind of sophistication, an acknowledgment of basic fact. Although I never could share that attitude, I found it refreshing.

All this mulling was useless, and I shook myself out of it. To business then, and the first item was the parents of Laura Jane. But I waited an instant. The June sun, lowering now, lay kind on the land, like a warm hand. To the west the mountains were shadowed, rising blue and black, wearing snow patches on gullied slopes. Closer, down the slope from the house, lay the new town of Overthrust. It had sprung up in my absence, the consequence of an oil strike. A combination of shacks, cabins, board-fronted stores and ambitious buildings of buff brick, it was raw and alien to this foothill country. It boasted it would put the county seat in the shade. Wrong. Oil settlements came and went, hustling with lease hounds, geologists, roughnecks, foremen, managers and slim typists in high heels, and then they faded away to rocker arms and storage tanks and a handful of workmen.

I turned on the engine and eased the car down to the bridge. I knew where the Smitsons lived, and I knew their names, thanks to Halvor's earlier report. The house was small and white with green trim. A couple of dying petunias decorated the front. I rang the bell. The door opened and revealed an older woman dressed in rusty black. She sized me up out of discouraged eyes.

"Mrs. Smitson," I said, "my name is Jason Beard. I'm a deputy in the sheriff's office. May I come in?"

"What sheriff?"

"Chick Charleston, your sheriff."

"He already sent a man, and our girl not laid in her grave."

"I know. It's too bad."

She looked me up and down again. She had a large bosom and, from the look of her hips, a large behind. She moved back. "I guess all right."

Then she turned her head to say, "A man's here, Smitty."

The room I entered was clean and just fairly well furnished. Some wilting funeral flowers sat on a table. On a wall was a print of two horses, one black, one white, both frightened by lightning. This much I took in before Mrs. Smitson said, "This is my husband."

In an armchair a man huddled up as if condensing himself against pain. His blue shirt was too big for him. So were his suspendered pants. At the end of thin, bare arms his knuckles bulged like knobs. From them his fingers grew crooked. Raggedly cut, his hair went every which way. Altogether he reminded me of a last year's bird's nest.

I gave him a greeting and repeated my name.

"Can't shake your hand, Mister," he said. "Damned arthritis."

"Might as well take a chair," Mrs. Smitson told me. She put herself down in a rocker. I was right about her behind.

Seated, I said, "I know it's painful, answering questions again, but I want to find the man who did away with your daughter."

"Sure," Smitson said with no hope in his voice.

"So I have to go over the case again on the chance you've forgotten something that may be of help."

"We don't know nothin'," Smitson said. "Just what we been told."

"She was laid to rest just last week," Mrs. Smitson put in.

"She worked for the Overthrust Oil Company, didn't she?"

It was Mrs. Smitson who answered. "She went to business college. She was a good typist. Took shorthand, too. They liked her."

"A good girl all around, what you call a loving daughter," Smitson said.

Mrs. Smitson nodded. A couple of tears rolled from her forlorn eyes. "We couldn't have got along without her."

"Believe it or not," Smitson said, "I was a real man once. Outdoor work. Worked for the telephone company, worked on construction, worked on ranches, and they was glad to have me. Never made no big money, but it was regular. But by littles my joints swole and movin' hurt like hell." He laughed, a single rasping sound like the voice of a night bird. "You see me now. Not worth a shit."

"You wouldn't talk that way if she was here, Smitty."

"I guess the man understands."

"When did you get alarmed at her absence?"

"We didn't really," Mrs. Smitson answered. "She what you call moonlighted. That was at Madame Simone's." Her eyes flickered to her husband. "She was so pretty. She posed, you know. She was a model." Her eyes begged me to believe.

"Made good money, too," Smitson said. "And brought it home and helped us out. Jesus. It's bad days ahead." He brought an arm up, winced, and laid it back.

"We didn't worry about her," Mrs. Smitson went

on. "Sometimes she called to say what her plans were. Sometimes she didn't. Sometimes, if she worked late, she spent the night at Madame Simone's. But she always turned up here, regular. So we didn't worry. It's only a hop, skip and jump, here to Madame Simone's."

"The first you knew about her death then—"

"Was when the officers came and told us. Oh, what a day!" She began to sob.

I waited until she wiped her eyes with the heels of her hands. "Is there anything you didn't tell the deputy who was here before me?"

"We answered his questions same as with you," Smitson told me.

"But it was like he didn't expect much from us," Mrs. Smitson said. "So you might say the talk was short and sweet."

"So there was something?"

Mrs. Smitson had control of herself now. "You know, with her gone and the funeral and all, things go out of your head." She made a little gesture, asking understanding.

"All the same," Smitson put in, "we would have told him if he'd asked."

"Yes, what was it?"

"A sapphire."

"I'll tell him, Smitty. A gold pin with a big sapphire in it. She wore it all the time, except of course at night."

"Big as a hazel nut, almost. A Yogo, they called it. Cornflower blue Yogo."

Mrs. Smitson said, "It was give to her out of kindness by some gentleman she knew."

"His name?"

"She never would tell."

I looked from one to the other. "You're saying it was gone when she was found?"

"Yeah," Smitson answered. "Stole, I guess. We've looked at her purse and what she had in it and the dress she wore, but no sapphire. Worth a pretty penny, too."

"You're sure?"

"Sure she had it." Smitson laughed his bird cry again. "And sure it's gone bye-bye. There was money in her purse, too, money she was likely going to turn over to us. It's ours as it is. Last of it."

"With her dead it's kind of like losing our own lives," Mrs. Smitson said and began crying again.

"I'll be in touch," I told them and let myself out the door, chalking up another miss for Halvor.

The sun was gone now, leaving a blaze in the northwest sky. My mother would heat up something if I went home, but home was thirty miles away, and I chose not to trouble her. I drove into the little town and ate at a counter, damning all fry cooks. When they die, forget the embalming fluid. Use grease.

3

I woke up early and lay quiet, letting my mind drift. Just three days back in Midbury, and here I was again on Sheriff Chick Charleston's staff and again assigned to a murder case. I had expected to spend an idle summer, then move to Portland, where a good position, opening in the fall, awaited me in the police department. I felt qualified for it. I had studied psychology, abnormal psychology, criminology and related subjects and had been to FBI school. On the side, for pleasure, I had enrolled in a good many classes in English. What's more, I had a degree.

The day after my arrival Charleston showed up. My mother liked him, as I did, and insisted on his having coffee and cookies. Yet she regarded him a little warily, fearing he might talk me into something dangerous.

He sat quietly, munching a cookie. He was a well set-up man, weighing perhaps 180 with no fat. He was friendly enough but much of the time, until he smiled, appeared thoughtful and impassive. The smile did wonders. He was well into his third four-year term as sheriff and would have retired, not needing the money, but for public insistence. His was a true case of the office seeking the man.

Watching him eat and drink, I recalled my long association with him. As a high-schooler I had hung around his office and later, mostly during college vacations, had served as his deputy, always as it happened in cases of murder.

At last he got around to the subject. "You've heard of the murder, I suppose?"

"Here and there."

"It's a difficult case, Jase, and, as usual, I'm shorthanded."

"I figured on loafing for a while, then going to Portland to work."

"Good job?"

"With the police department. I won't be pounding the pavement."

Mother, who had been fluttering around while watching us, said to him, "He needs a rest."

Her concern always made me a little obstinate.

"I see." Charleston smiled at her. "A little more field work might add to his credentials."

"He's had plenty of that," she answered.

"Quiet, Mother, please," I said and put out a hand to touch her.

"It was a chance." Charleston rose. "Thanks for the coffee and cookies, Mrs. Beard."

He was making for the door when I told him, "I don't like to turn you down."

"It's all right, Jase."

"Any leads in the case?"

"Not a one. Not a blessed one."

"I might look over what you have."

I was hooked. You might even say I was conned.

So here I was lolling in bed when I'd better roll out of it.

I was still in good time. I did my chores in the bathroom, ate breakfast while Mother fussed over me, and went to the office. Ike Doolittle perched near the switchboard close to the radio transmitter. Sheriff Charleston had taken to calling the person on the board the watch commander, a phrase he had probably picked up from a book.

Ike said, "Morning, Jase. No business here. Not a towel wet."

It was a temptation to think of him as elfin, yet I

knew better. Once, in my defense, he had subdued a man much bigger than he was.

I answered, "Good."

I went to the inner office and sat down at the typewriter. There was plenty to report. While I was typing Charleston came in. Somehow he always managed to look as if he had just been outfitted for his role. Polished boots, creased pants, short jacket and sand-colored hat without a stain. He said, "Bright and early must mean you found something?"

"Something."

"Give me the gist of it."

So I turned from the machine and sat at the office side of his desk. I told him about the fracas at Madame Simone's and the missing sapphire.

He tapped on his desk with the end of a pencil. "That's something all right. Halvor missed both leads." His face bore the traces of a frown.

I said, "Halvor's all right."

"Yep, in his place. That's why I keep him on." Charleston put down the pencil and rested his hands on the desk. "There was nothing else to do, Jase. I had to be in court. Doolittle was investigating some cattle thefts over east. You remember Monk Fitzroy?"

"Used to be stationed at Petroleum."

"Yes. Petroleum folded, you know. Everybody moved to Overthrust. Some buildings relocated, too. So I brought Monk in, and then he up and died. The last man I hired I had to fire. Halvor was all I had for the murder case." He pointed at me. "I'm damn glad to have you, boy."

"Thanks. There's a long way to go yet."

"I know. That's the gist, huh? Nothing else?"

"Not of real importance. It's beside the point, but what gets me is that the Smitsons knew the girl was whoring and almost seemed to approve. Of course she supported them."

"Didn't forget her ma and pa."

"No. They depended on her. Her father's a cripple. Even so, they seemed as much upset about the end of the handouts as about her death."

Charleston sighed. "I suppose it figures. Poverty's a stinking thing. It mixes up values. It doesn't team up with purity. What's a little whoring, what's death, when the belly's empty. I think Laura Jane was quite a girl."

"She must have been quite a dish, too. A fight over her and a sapphire for her. You know any Fords in the county?"

"Ford?" He shook his head. "Must be new."

"I'll find out. That's next. And I want to locate the man who gave her the sapphire."

"Doubtful suspect, isn't he?"

"Who knows?"

"It's your case, Jase."

I went back to the typewriter. When I was done, I laid my report on his desk and left the office. I scanned the list of registered electors. No Ford. I studied the assessment sheets. I went to the treasurer's office and asked about automobile licenses. Ford was just a name for machines.

It was past noon when I finished, and I went to the Commercial Cafe for a sandwich. No fried hamburger, thanks. Just a bacon, lettuce and tomato.

In front of the bank Mike Day, the head man, stopped me and shook hands. He was one of the few acquaintances I hadn't seen since my return. "How are you, Jason boy? In the pink, I see. Back bloodhounding, so the little bird says."

"Can't pick up a scent."

"Come inside. I want you to meet my nephew, Roland Day. Just out of college. Knows bookkeeping, accounting, banking practices, and all that. He'll take a load off of me."

So far as I knew the only load Mike Day ever carried was his own weight.

The man behind the railing was as young or younger than I. He was a well set-up young fellow with a good carriage, broad shoulders and very light hair parted at the side. He was as pale as the paper on his desk. He

wore tinted glasses, and behind them I caught the
glimmer of very light blue eyes. An albino, I thought,
or close to it. His shake was firm, and his smile good.

I welcomed him and wished him the best of luck
and at the door turned back and asked if they had a
Ford among their depositors. "Wished I did," Mike
Day said. "Like a Ford name of Henry." I waved away
their curiosity.

Bob Studebaker chewed on a toothpick at the Bar
Star Saloon. He had two customers. No one there knew
a man by the name of Ford. "What's the idea?" Studebaker
asked. "He in trouble?"

"How can he be? He doesn't exist."

On a far-out hunch I went to see Miss Phoebe
Akers. For years she had been selling low-priced orna-
ments like pins and bracelets and earrings and a few
good jewels in her office in the Jackson Hotel. For good
reason she was known as a talker.

"Good afternoon, Miss Akers," I said.

"Goodness me, if it isn't Jason Beard! A sight for
sore eyes."

We chatted or, rather, she talked, and then I said,
"How you fixed for sapphires?"

"Why, Jason, you got a girl!"

"I'm old enough."

"And good-looking enough. Sure, I have sapphires,
genuine Yogos." She produced a tray. "Take a peek."

I did so and said, "I wanted a big one."

"You're sure enough in love. I don't sell many large
stones. On account of the price, you know."

"Yes."

"Two, three weeks ago, I had a wonderful one. I
thought I'd never sell it. Then a man came along, a
stranger, and bought it right off the bat. No bargaining.
No questions. Paid cash."

"Was his name Ford?"

"Ford? No. I don't know any Fords. Let me think.
Oh, yes." She ran a finger down a ledger. "Here we are.
Gerald Fenner. That's all he told me, just his name.
Since then, inquiring around, you know, but really not

being nosy, I found he's a big-time lawyer, staying at
Overthrust for a few months. I suppose he's working on
deeds or transfers or leases or something. Those oil
companies and their lawyers, my! But you wanted a
sapphire, and here I am jabbering away."

"Not at all," I answered. "Nice to talk to you. Keep
in touch just in case."

It was only a little after midafternoon, early enough
for a trip to Overthrust and an interview. I debated
going. Things, one thing at least, had come along too
easily, and easy answers weren't to be trusted. A long
shot could come home first and then be disqualified.

I walked back to the courthouse and took an official
car. In forty minutes I was at Overthrust again. A
gas-station pumper said sure, he knew Mr. Fenner. Had
an office in the new brick building yonder.

He wasn't on the first floor. It was occupied by the
offices of the Overthrust Oil Company. A man there
said he could be found upstairs, first door to the right. I
climbed the stairs and arrived at the door. It was
unmarked. Inside, a wispy girl with glasses and the look
of male neglect asked me my business.

"I'll tell Mr. Fenner that," I said. "My name is
Jason Beard."

"You don't have an appointment?"

"Sorry. Just say I'm investigating a jewel theft."

"A jewel theft! What in the world?"

"I'm a deputy sheriff."

She breathed out a deep breath. Under it she
might have been saying, "Of all the crazy things!"

She went into the inner office, came right back and
told me, "He'll see you."

The office was deep-carpeted in rust. Some nice
prints hung on the wall. Mr. Fenner rose from behind a
mahogany desk and said, "Good afternoon, Mr. Beard."
I took him to be in his fifties. He wore a gray three-
piece suit and a blue tie. He stood erect, his head up,
his face unrevealing but not unfriendly. He had dignity
about him and something of the air of the aristocrat.
Not that I really knew any aristocrats.

"Please have a chair," he said, seating himself. "Now what's all this about a jewel theft? It can hardly concern me."

"Only incidentally if at all."

"Proceed."

"The stone in question is a big sapphire."

"And there's some doubt about ownership—about provenance?"

"No, sir. Nothing like that."

"What then? Tell me."

"Mr. Fenner," I said, "I don't know that you fit into the case at all. I'm working blind. I would ask your pardon except that you may be able to help me. I hope you will."

"That talk behind you, let's get down to cases?"

"As you know, a young girl was killed on the edge of town a few days ago, raped and strangled. It was her custom to wear a big sapphire in a setting of gold."

He sat still, unmoving, without a flicker of face or tremor of hands. I thought of rigidity. "What about it?"

"It's missing."

"Hardly my concern, Mr. Beard."

"In a way it may be. I think you gave the pin to the little prostitute."

"I hate that word," he said, flinging out an arm as if to thrust it away.

I waited. He arose slowly and took a step or two, his hands clasped behind him. His head, once so upright, was bent. He said, not turning to me, "I don't see—"

"It may be none of my business," I said for him, "but I intend to find out."

He went, stooping, back to his chair. "Some things are private. Some things are confidential."

"I keep them that way unless they come into a case."

"And discussing them casts false lights. It makes them small. Makes them ugly. It distorts truth."

"Yes, sir."

He sat down, and his hands came out in slow

explanation. "Mr. Beard, I'm a married man, but only in a sense. My wife is a sick woman, long since past any interest in men, including me except that she depends on me and rightly so. I support her. See that she gets the best of attention. But, Mr. Beard, I'm a man. As such I know the needs of the spirit and the hungers of the flesh."

That was a fancy way of putting it, but he meant every word.

Again I waited.

"It came about that I met Laura Jane. It doesn't matter how. She was a splendid girl. I gave her the pin."

"It was quite a gift."

"She was quite a girl."

"No quarrels?"

"Good Lord, no! She was a good and gentle girl, a tender girl. She had time and concern for me."

I didn't say she must have liked what he gave her, too.

He went on, "Until some years have passed, you can't know what the loving attention of a young girl means to an older man. You can't know." His head moved, slow with remembrance. "She cared for me. I am sure she cared for me." A pause then. "Yes." The single word dropped toward his desk. "Yes."

I went out quietly. Aristocrats had a right to privacy, too.

4

It happened in all businesses, professions and public services that I knew anything about—the lulls between storms. The sheriff's office was having one now; and Charleston, Ike Doolittle and I were loafing in Old Doc Yak's office, along with Doc himself and Felix Underwood, the town mortician.

It had become something of a habit with a few of Doc's friends, to drop in his place of an evening if time permitted. One missing member now was Bob Studebaker, who often came in for a quiet drink away from his bar and juke boxes. We had glasses in our hands. A bottle of whiskey and a pitcher of water rested on Doc's desk.

We were, I supposed, a queer assortment, brought together through years of association and sometimes common interests.

Old Doc Yak properly was Dr. Gaylord Summerville, but Doc Yak was the name of an early-day cartoon character, and he had acquired it. Most people now would have had to think twice to address him correctly. Crusty as a cracker, he was the world's worst driver and the last doctor to accept death, natural or violent. There was nothing meek about Doc.

As we sat, waiting for drink to promote talk, I thought of the change that was overtaking Felix Underwood. Once rather free and easy except at funerals, he was becoming stuffy, perhaps because of a growing bankroll. I flirted with the idea of the relationship between property and propriety.

I was feeling worthless. All my leads had petered out. I had questioned Madame Simone's friendly sheriff. No help there. I had talked to his deputies. Sure, there had been a little fracas at Madame's house, but they had straightened it out and sent the man on his way. Name? No one remembered.

"By my lights she was a good girl," Charleston was saying. He was never quite easy away from his work though he had no real reason to fret now. Sure, he had put a new man on the board—one Kenneth Cole from Titusville—but he was being coached by Blanche Burton, an old watch-commander hand.

A breeze stirred a curtain in an open window. June in Montana, I thought, a time of bluster and sunshine and long light. Not for an hour would Doc have to switch on a lamp. I smelled the first fragrance of lilacs.

Charleston added after a pause, "She took care of her mother and father."

"All the same, she was selling it," Underwood answered Charleston. He had grown a little fleshy, thanks to a good life and dead bodies.

"For Christ's sake," Doc Yak replied, "that damns her to you, huh? You and your embalmed moralities."

He swept out an arm as if asking the office and heaven to bear witness. "Listen to the voice of the righteous, but heed not. All is foolishness."

Doc had enlarged his quarters by taking out the partition between the waiting room and the bedroom where he used sometimes to put patients. Patients were few these days. Some older ones swore by him and fought shy of the two new doctors. Neither did they like the new hospital. Declining practice pleased Doc. He was trying to retire, though he held on to the job of coroner.

Charleston went on, softly:

> Take her up tenderly
> Lift her with care;
> Fashioned so slenderly,
> Young, and so fair!

"*Bridge of Sighs*," Doolittle said. It was a game they played, each trying to stump the other with a literary reference. Doolittle gave a satisfied, small smile. Slumped in a leather chair, he appeared even smaller than he was, but, looking at him, I remembered that a tough customer, being locked into a cell, had characterized him as hell on wheels.

"I wouldn't know about that fair business," Underwood said. "I didn't get the job. That damn upstart town! Overthrust! They'll find out same way we found out when we bragged up Midbury as the coal capital of Montana. Shit. Came a soft market for coal and our coal turned out poor, and here we are like always.

"And there's you, Charleston," he went on, his indignation spilling over. "Jase, here, would be pitching professional ball if he hadn't hurt his hand helping you." He was a baseball nut and couldn't forget that a bullet had stiffened my pitching hand maybe half a dozen or more years ago.

"What's that got to do with fair?" Doc asked him. "Me, I examined the body. Even choked she was pretty, or had been." He shook his head. Age had seamed and contracted his face. It might have been the face of a turtle, except that his head and eyes flicked around like a chipmunk's. "The choker had big hands, but that doesn't help you, Jase. Who doesn't have big hands in this clodhopper country?"

Underwood returned to his standards. "A good-looking girl doesn't have to whore if she has any sense in her head." He seconded himself with a drink.

"Felix," Doc said, "a salute to your vision. And now, brothers and sisters, let us turn the page and sing of the patent-medicine hawkers. There's whoring of a high order. Thanks to law, they are somewhat restrained these days, but they are the get of wenchers and sluts."

"Aw, bull, Doc. Where's the connection between companies and whores?" Felix spoke with good nature. He was a hard man to offend.

"Whores, quacks, same thing," Doc answered. "No damn field has so many fornicators in it as the health business. Look what the patent-medicine people used to do. Doped their tonics and brews with cocaine or whatever. Once they had their customers hooked, they came along with cures, also doped. Sold their souls for profit. It's the damn truth. What say, there, Brother Underwood?"

"Whoring is whoring."

"I ask you, I ask you in all conscience, which is the worse, a little nookie or slavery to drugs? Not," he added, "that I think the first item is bad."

"You mean, speaking from memory," Doolittle put in.

"Your inference is as infirm as your stature is small," Doc answered him in faked offense. "A man's a man until he dies."

Now Doolittle quoted:

> The grave's a fine and private place,
> But none, I think, do there embrace.

Doolittle looked at Charleston, who said, "Andrew Marvell."

So far the game was tied.

To keep Doc going I said, "But that's in the past? The doped cures and all?"

"Better now, sure. But you still find dangerous stuff being peddled, and not by the patent people alone. So-called reputable companies put out bad stuff. When it's caught up with and stopped, it's too late for the victims. They can sue if they're alive, but shit."

"Older generations had some funny ideas," Charleston said. "When one of us kids had a sore throat or croup, our mother would take an old stocking, line it with raw bacon, sprinkle the bacon with pepper, and tie the stocking around the sore neck. Worked, too."

"Some old practices did," Doc said. "More didn't. But if the patient thought he was better, then by God he was." Doc drank again. "I get called on for some old, crazy items now and then. Cubebs, for instance."

I asked, "Cubebs?"

"Cigarettes made out of medicated peppers. Anyhow they smelled medicated. Then there was antiphlogistine, sometimes called Denver Mud. It was mud all right, smooth mud with perfume in it. Used like a mustard plaster."

"Did it work?" Doolittle asked.

"As long as people thought so, sure. You ever hear of asafoetida? Parents used to tie it in a piece of rag and hang it from strings around the kids' necks. Supposed to ward off germs like scarlet fever."

"Good disinfectant?" Felix asked.

"Nope. It smelled so bad any self-respecting germ was supposed to stay clear. Jesus, what a stench! A dog would puke."

We took time to sip at our drinks. Doc licked his lips and went on, full of himself thanks to what he had had. "You go back and you find all kinds of claims. The poor damn people didn't know any better. Medicine was bound up with folklore, with witchery, superstition and what not. Sometimes it wasn't so far off the mark, though. Take foxglove. Take deadly nightshade. Take henbane. All poisonous. And from them these days we get digitalis, we get belladonna, we get hyoscine."

Doolittle asked, "What's hyoscine?"

"Questions. Questions. That's all I get."

"Come off it, Doc," Doolittle told him. "Every one of those words had a question mark after it. You ask questions so we'll ask questions."

Doc grinned an evil, turtle grin. "Smart ass. If ever you are taken with child and know the pains of delivery, ask for hyoscine. That's twilight sleep."

"Case closed. Any other benefits?"

"Lots of them. It was the willow gave us the idea for aspirin." Doc rubbed his jaw. "The things patients ask for, though. Just lately a man wanted nitrate of potassium."

Doc knew that someone would ask what that was, and Underwood did.

"It's commonly known as saltpeter."

I saw Charleston look up.

"That works against sex, huh?"

"Supposed to suppress the instinct. Supposed to dull desire. Been used in the army and navy and prisons. Maybe still is. I can't swear to results except it makes a man piss."

"Who in hell would ask for that?" Underwood said, curiosity getting the upper hand of morality.

"You know better, Felix. That's confidential."

"And you prescribed it?"

"Yep, but no need to. Anyone can buy it. It's just that a prescription gives a sort of legitimacy to the purchase. Makes it all kosher. Doctor's orders."

The telephone rang then. The caller wanted Charleston. After listening, Charleston turned to me. "Report of a rustled calf. We can't do anything tonight. Still, I'll run along."

I went out with him.

5

Doolittle was on the board when I entered the office next morning.

"Hey," I said. "How come? Not your turn."

Doolittle grinned. "I'm just spellin' Halvor. He's in what you might call the gentlemen's room, cheerin' peristalsis on."

I grinned back. A drifter before he got to be deputy, Doolittle had educated himself by reading every book he could get his hands on. He could make me, with my degree, feel ignorant, not meaning to.

Charleston was at his desk, my report before him. He motioned me to sit down. "This Gerald Fenner," he said, looking up. "He's on the level?"

"I'd bet on it."

"A middle-aged man in the chancy years when he's trying to get hold of what he's losing. He could be mean if the girl turned against him."

"I can't figure it that way."

He laid the report to one side. "Old Mr. Gates— he's the one who reported the calf rustling last night— he's on the way in. Should be here any minute. Better stick around unless you have something better to do."

"My stock of inspiration ran out."

It was a little short of an hour before Gates entered. He was a man maybe of sixty-five with stooped shoulders, a face that had been patterned by wind, and eyes that distance had given a squint. We shook hands with him.

After he sat down, he said, "Thought I might as well come in and give you the dope."

Charleston made a little tent of his hands and rested them on the desk. "One calf missing?"

"Nope. Two. I don't run much stock and I keep tally. I know who took 'em, too."

We waited.

Gates pointed a finger at Charleston. It was deformed, as if it had been caught sometime between saddle horn and dallied rope. "There's a squatter in Chicken Coulee not so far from me. You know the place. It's government land and under lease but no good for anything and so nobody kicks about his old camper. A crick runs through it, but it's wore itself so deep that cattle can't get down to water, and there's maybe one spear of grass to every square yard. You savvy?"

"Sure. Go on."

"So the damn man squats there in a camper that must have been first off the line, and with him's a woman that's all tangle and angle iron. I know. I saw them."

Charleston got out one of the few cigars he permitted himself, offered another to Gates, and lighted them both. "What makes you suspect him outside of what you've said?"

"What they call process of elimination. Who the hell else would make off with my stock?"

"Your elimination cuts a wide swathe. It's hardly conclusive."

"Think so, do you? What they livin' on, savin' maybe a rabbit or two, allowin' just maybe for a deer that he's poached? I tell you, I saw 'em."

Charleston blew out a thin stream of smoke. "You braced him, then?"

Gates made a little helpless gesture with his hands. "Tried to, but he run me off. I don't carry a gun. Never did. And I'm too old to fight, anyhow too old for that bastard."

"What's he like?"

"Like a goddamn thief."

"His looks, I mean."

"Young, big and strong, and he's all hair, like as if his neck just haired out."

Charleston straightened in his chair. "It's not a lot to go on, but we'll look into it."

"Look and learn, goddamnit."

"What's the man's name?"

"I wouldn't know, except I heard the woman call out when he made like to fight me. 'Mefford,' she told him. 'Stop it. You'll get your ass burned.' Them were her exact, lady-like words."

After Gates had gone Charleston said, "We could nose around, I suppose, just to show Gates we're on the job, but it would be a waste of time. No evidence, nothing to justify a search warrant. And Mefford, if it is Mefford, wouldn't leave hair or hide of the calves around." He looked at his watch. "Early for lunch, but I'm hungry."

At the board Halvor told us, "Old Mrs. Wilcox had her house broken into. Doolittle said not to bother you. He'd take it."

We had sandwiches at the Jackson Hotel. I said, chewing the last bite, "I think I'll go to the high school."

"School's out."

"But the principal may be around. What's his name?"

"Parsons. Alfred Parsons. But why see him?"

"Background on Laura Jane Smitson. She probably went to high school here."

Charleston gave a little grin. "That's what I might call shooting in the dark."

"The dark is all there is to shoot at."

"Go on, Jase. You might bring down a night bird."

I walked to the high school that warm afternoon. The sun promised eternal summer, but I knew June in Montana. The wind might rage tomorrow, or the sky darken and clouds drench the land. Never a dull moment, from drouth to flood. People in Montana had to like weather.

A girl was just going out as I entered the high school. She was a trim and pretty thing, dressed in a white blouse and gray skirt. I asked, "Miss, could you direct me to the principal's office? Do you know whether he's in?"

In a voice that was music she answered to my surprise, "He just came in, Mr. Beard. Walk down the hall, turn right, and you'll see the office."

I thanked her, not asking how it was that she knew my name.

I knocked at the office door and was told to come in. Mr. Parsons rose from his desk and smiled largely. He was a beaming man with a beginning pot. It occurred to me that it took a lot of beaming to endure high-schoolers.

"My name is Jason Beard," I told him. We shook hands. "Who was that nice young girl who directed me to the office? She knew me."

"That must have been Virginia Stuart. You haven't heard of her?"

"Should I have? I don't know. I just returned to town."

"You will hear of her. She's the prize. She's a well-mannered, thoroughly decent young lady with a voice that God gives to few."

"She's a singer?"

Parsons stuck out his arms as if to embrace an unembraceable talent. "As fine a soprano as these ears ever heard. She's practicing now for the state festival, where she'll win hands down. And she's generous with her gifts. She gave a recital at the school last Christmas and another at graduation. Everybody came. They were uplifted. What a voice!"

I had heard enough of her, but Parsons wasn't through. "Her father is Duncan Stuart, as staid a Scotsman as you'll ever meet. That's where she gets her manners and principles."

"It sounds as if she were a person apart. No schoolgirl antics?"

"Oh, she dates a bit, not much. Lately I've seen her a time or two with that young man at the bank, but it can't be anything serious."

"I see, but I came to ask you—"

"Please." Mr. Parsons delayed me with an uplifted hand. "She is training under a man from the city, but I doubt he's good enough. He comes twice a week, and some people show up just to hear her practice. After graduation she'll go east, to Juilliard perhaps. The town is so proud of her that it's gathering a fund to see her through. The bank, under Mr. Mike Day, started the idea and the contributions with a gift of a thousand dollars. Mr. Stuart is a proud man but not really well off. He's had to swallow his pride."

"I'd like to hear her."

Mr. Parsons nodded. "I'm forgetting your purpose." He sat back waiting, his fingers intertwined on his belly.

"Of course you've heard of the murder at Overthrust, the murder of one Laura Jane Smitson?"

"Indeed I have. What a pity! And what a life she seems to have led!"

"You knew her?"

"Of course. She was a student here. She dropped out after her sophomore year. That was three years ago, I believe."

"What kind of a girl was she?"

"A very decent student, not brilliant but genuinely competent. I understand she went then to business college. It was family finances, I gather, that caused her to leave here."

"Was she—let me see—wild at all? No escapades? No scandals?"

"None whatever, which is more than you can say of some students."

"You back up what I've been led to believe about her. But what about her friends, any wild ones in the group?"

"Not to my knowledge. I believe she had few friends, perhaps because she had to dress rather poorly. Shabbiness—it wasn't quite that—begets few friendships." Mr. Parsons breathed with satisfaction as if he had uttered truth in a nutshell.

"No run-ins, then? Not with a roughneck whose name might be Ford?"

"No. In my time there's never been a Ford enrolled here."

I rose and thanked him. He beamed his goodbye as I said, "I'm just turning over stones, without any luck."

6

"Mr. Charleston had to go out," Ken Cole on watch command told me the next morning. "Be back by noon or so."

Cole—elevated by Doolittle to King Cole—seemed to be fitting in all right. He was a dark-skinned man, maybe a year or two older than I, with brown mournful eyes but a cheerful enough air. He had on a black shirt and black pants, and I said to kid him, "Jack Palance killed any taxpayers today?"

Even dark-skinned men can flush. He answered, "Black isn't a bad color when it comes to stocking shelves and bagging groceries. I worked in a store, and these are the best I have. I can't hardly wait for my uniform."

"Forget I said it. I was just joshing. The sheriff isn't too strong for up-to-snuff uniforms. Thinks they might lead to uniformity of mind." I wore a short, blue-gray jacket with trousers to match but hadn't put on a tie.

I went back to type up my report. That didn't take long, so for a while I sat quiet and tried to make what I knew tell me something. It didn't. I went back to Cole, who was fiddling with a camera. A tripod and second camera stood in a corner.

"Nothing important here," he said. "One lost dog. A complaint about county kids running over private lawns on their way to school."

"You made notes just the same?" I was trying to help him.

"Sure. I didn't forget."

"You a photographer?"

"Kind of. I think that's why I got the job."

"One of the reasons."

"That and maybe an interest in police work."

I wandered back. On Charleston's desk was a copy of *Komongo*. I got interested in the pros and cons of faith and science.

Charleston came in at noon, saying "Pisswillie." It was a term of his for the trifling or vexing. "Sorry to hold you up, Jase," he said.

"You didn't. I wasn't going anywhere. There's my report."

He sat down and interlocked his fingers and cast a keen eye on me. "I have a straw to grab at."

"Yes, sir."

He untwined his fingers and took up a pencil and studied it. Then he said, "Mefford. Mefford. Ford. Mr. Ford—Mefford."

It took a minute for me to understand. "That's a long rope to throw."

"Yep. But I want that man brought in."

"I could go out and question him."

"Not from what we hear. There he'd be in his element. I want him in mine."

"All right."

"Maybe I'd better send a man with you."

I said, "I can handle it myself."

That's what I thought.

I had a bite of lunch and set out for Chicken Coulee. I knew where it was, and I knew a short cut. Roving kids learn geography.

A storm was building up in the west. Not rain clouds, I thought. Too much light gray. But June was early times for hail. The wind pushed at the car when I turned from the highway to a rough, graded road.

The wind came first, then charges of hail as big as pigeon eggs. I turned the car around to save the windshield. I couldn't hear the engine for the hard thunder on the roof. The green fields turned white. I could run for cover, but where was it?

Then all at once the storm was over, and the sun came out, shining on the beaten fields. Somehow the glass in the car was unbroken, but the roof and hood might have been hit by a ball-peen hammer. I turned the machine around and drove on.

A back wheel slipped off the greasy road and sank to the hub. Rocking back and forth just dug a trench. Police cars always carried a blanket and shovel. I got busy with the shovel. After a hard hour I was on the way again.

Chicken Coulee had escaped the storm. An old camper stood on the high bank of a stream, and a man stood beside it. A gaunt woman looked out the door.

I left the car, walked toward the man and asked, "Are you Mr. Mefford?"

The description I had received fitted him. He was big and hairy, dressed in dirty work clothes. The woman had taken a step from the camper.

He asked, "What's it to you?"

"The sheriff wants to talk to you."

"I don't see no sheriff."

"I'm a deputy. My name's Beard."

He began advancing on me. I stood my ground. "If your fuckin' sheriff wants to talk to me, let him come and do it."

"No, sir. That's not the way he wants it."

"Two different things, what he wants and what he gets." He took two steps and swung.

It was a wild and awkward punch, and I thought, slipping it, that I had no need for fancy stuff. I hit him hard with a left and right.

They shook him, and a roar came out of him. He tried to close in, wanting to grapple. This time I hit him harder, left and right, and he teetered and went down.

I started putting on handcuffs. Too late, I glimpsed the swing of something dark. It hit me, the edge of a frying pan, I learned later. I learned a lot of things later.

*   *   *

What I have to report now comes from dredged-up memory, from what others said and said I did. I was seeing through a wall of water. I was hearing through a waterfall.

"Try to sit up, please, Mr. Beard." They were the first words. "Lean on my shoulder. Ain't far to help."

They were just sounds without meaning, heard above a rumble that might be in my head. It had teeth and claws in it.

Then, it seemed to me, I sat in a chair, and a mist clouded my eyes and a woman's face swam in it.

"Was he sick, Omar?"

"No'm."

"Sit up, Jason. He's red in the face, Omar. Help hold him. Now, Jason, look me in the eyes." Her eyes were enormous. I tried to look at her through the pain in my head. She was putting something on the side of my skull. I got a hand up and felt cloth.

"Sheriff," I think I said. "Sheriff."

"I'll telephone. Don't worry. Now don't you go to sleep yet. You have to sit up for a while. Omar, help him." A hand was soft on my forehead.

Then I was in bed, and pain clouded my brain, and the hand kept trying to soothe me, and a voice was saying over and over, "You'll be all right. You'll be all right. Hear me, Jason?"

Next, there were two men in the room, and one of them raised me to look, and I remember he said, "Couldn't have done better myself, Miss. One hell of a headache he's having, I'll bet. Keep talking to him after I leave. Here's some pills with directions."

Then the voice again, "Don't go clear to sleep. Not yet. Hear me, Jason? Hear me?"

When I came to, more or less, the sun was shining. It was Anita Dutton who entered the room, Anita, the girl I had courted and lost and would always want. "Oh, you're awake," she said. "Good morning. How are you now?"

"All right," I answered, though I wasn't. "I have to report."

"The sheriff was here last night. So was Doc Yak. They ordered rest." She put a glass of water on a bedside table, first offering it to me. Then she began straightening the covers.

"But I have to get out," I said.

My one-time girl friend, forever in memory. But, cold as the Arctic, she had shut the door on me after I found it was her dotty old grandfather who had killed a man by senile mistake. I hadn't seen her since. The grandfather had died in custodial care. Already, I thought, she was remembering. No more hands on my head. No more soft words.

"I'm damn sorry to bother you," I told her. "God knows I didn't mean to."

"It's a person's duty to help. I was glad to do it. Now lie still."

When Charleston and Doc Yak appeared, I was sitting up in bed. Charleston's first anxious look turned into a grin. "By the gods, Jason, you're a tough man. How you feeling? Feel like reporting?"

Doc Yak broke in, "Goddamn you, Charleston. Can't wait to let me examine the patient." He looked me in the eyes, took my blood pressure and temperature, and said, his mouth twisted, "I'm afraid he'll live."

Omar Test, Anita's man of all work, the one who had found me by the roadside, peeked in to say, "Glad you're better, Mr. Beard. Excuse me. Got chores to do."

So, as best I remember, I gave Charleston my report.

He said, "We found your car under that old, condemned bridge. I've had a man on watch in case they tried to run. They're still there. Now we'll bring those jokers in."

"Not yet, please," I asked him. "Make it tomorrow. I want to be on hand."

Charleston scratched his head. "I'll have to keep a man on lookout. That's stretching it thin."

"But it's my case." I don't know why I insisted on returning to that forlorn camper and its shoddy inhabitants. Pride, maybe, or a return to the scene of the crime.

"What say, Doc?" Charleston asked.

"By tomorrow he'll be half-assed ready, the damn fool." Doc always showed affection through abuse. He gave me a shot, said to Anita, "He could stand a bowl of soup."

"There's my mother," I said to Charleston.

"Don't worry. I'll see her. I'll reassure her." Trying to reassure my mother would be like trying to placate a she-bear.

I ate the soup and fell asleep again, feeling wretched and unwelcome.

The sun was down when Anita came in with scrambled eggs, toast and coffee. "Afterward take a pill for a good night's sleep."

I followed orders.

In the morning my headache was gone. The only sign of hurt was a bandage on my temple. I got out of bed and dressed.

When I walked into the kitchen, Anita, standing at the stove, said, "Up to some breakfast?"

I was.

And I was wanting to get out, away from the house, away from Anita, away from the bad memories I had awakened.

I asked, "Did Mr. Charleston say when he was coming back?"

"I hear him pulling up now."

I stammered my thanks to Anita. Before I got to the car, she called me back, half-closed the door on us, and kissed me. "That's forgiveness," she said.

7

Ike Doolittle was in the car with Charleston. He threw a keen glance at me and said, "Ever see such a bright face?" Then he began quoting. "'Lasca used to ride on a mouse-gray mustang close by my side.'"

Grinning, Charleston chimed in, "'She would hunger that I might eat. Would take the bitter and leave me the sweet.'"

They were choosing what they considered appropriate lines from a piece of verse I remembered. For an instant I was back in boyhood and heard my father reading it to me. In my mind were the concluding words to a number of stanzas. To put an end to this foolish kidding I said, "'In Texas, down by the Rio Grande.'" As a clincher I added, "Author, Frank Desprez."

That seemed to be that.

"Seriously, Jase," Charleston said, "you are to stay in the car. Take no part in the arrests. I put them off just so you could be present, present but not active."

"I'm almost as good as new."

"But not good enough. You heard me."

"Yes, sir. But if they have any sense, they'll be long gone."

"They're still there. I just heard from Ken Cole. He's on watch. I said he could take today off, so's to get settled in his new quarters, but when I mentioned this bird-dogging, he took it up like an English setter after grouse. He's to follow them and report if they take off."

I should have known better than to suggest Charleston had been careless.

The morning was bright, offering renewal of old promises. In the west the mountains reared, stone-blue except for a few patches of last winter's snow. The breeze blew the perfume of warming fields. I sat back, rich with recovery and climate.

Charleston didn't take the short cut, if he knew it. He was satisfied with a slow ride while his nose breathed in the good air. It took almost an hour to reach Chicken Coulee, where Charleston and Doolittle got out of the car. Doolittle stayed close to the side of it. Charleston stood for a minute, then said, "So that's how he's been getting around."

He had a better eye for detail than I. It took me a little while to spot a motorcycle half-hidden by a pile of wood.

Mefford emerged from the camper. The breeze caught a strand of his long hair and blew it forward across his beard. I was put in mind of a clump of slough grass. His woman came to the step, dressed in a cast-off man's shirt and ragged jeans.

Charleston and Mefford approached each other. Charleston said, "I'm the sheriff, Mefford, and I'm taking you in." I doubt Mefford saw Doolittle, still staying on the far side of the car, and thought he had just one man to deal with.

That one was enough. As Mefford bulled forward, Charleston stepped to meet him. In one flash of movement he brought a blackjack from his hip pocket and hit Mefford on the side of the head. Mefford went down without a word. I knew the blackjack was stuffed with sand, which made it lethal enough.

At the side of my vision I saw the woman scramble from the camper. She had a frying pan in her hand. Doolittle took care of her. He dodged under the swing of the pan, caught the woman around the ankles, yanked her feet from under her and set her on her butt with a thump that jarred the pan from her hand. I heard Doolittle say, "Awful sorry to upset you, ma'am."

She answered, getting up, "You're quicker than a

damn weasel. No need for the bracelets, Mr. Law. I'll come along."

Charleston was putting handcuffs on Mefford when Ken Cole drove up. "Just in time to miss the action," he said, coming from his car. "But I saw it pretty good, looking through a glass from the hill yonder."

"Put her in the car," Charleston said to Doolittle. "Ken and Jase can watch her. Then take a look in the camper. I have the warrant."

The woman came over willingly enough. In the car she said to me, "Looks like I fetched you a good one."

Charleston was half-dragging, half-lifting Mefford toward the car when Doolittle came out of the camper. "Don't have to believe it, but it's tidy inside," he said. "No sign of a calf hide."

Mefford had come to himself when we reached the sheriff's office. "Lock her up, Ike," Charleston said. "We'll hear from Mefford first."

We got settled in the office, Mefford on one side of the desk facing Charleston, me at the end of it taking notes, Doolittle watching from a seat in the corner. Mefford's hands had been freed from cuffs. Charleston cleared his throat, then said, "What do you have to say for yourself, Mefford? Do you want an attorney?"

Mefford answered, "Kiss my ass. You've half-killed me. Ain't that enough?"

"Get some aspirin, Doolittle."

Doolittle came back with two pills and a glass of water. Mefford knocked the glass from his hand. Ken Cole poked his head in and withdrew.

"Go ahead and suffer then," Charleston told Mefford. "It's all one to us."

"Kiss my ass."

Charleston dislikes back talk and vulgarity even more. He half-rose, shot a hand out and got a hold on the man's beard. He shook Mefford's head until I was dizzy. He sat back then. "Now we'll talk. Your case is open and shut. Assault and battery. Resisting an officer. Theft of an automobile. I can think of other charges. Attempted murder, for instance."

Mefford pointed at me. "He tackled me first. I was just fightin' him off."

"And leaving him for dead and stealing a car. Don't make me laugh."

Charleston wasn't laughing. He went on, "I'll get to something even more serious. You had a fight in a sporting house."

"Where?"

"You know where. Madame Simone's."

"Who says?"

"I have a witness who'll identify you."

"Since when is a fight in a whorehouse so serious?"

"There was a girl you wanted, one Laura Jane Smitson."

"Where's the harm in that?" Mefford straightened as if to declare himself. "She thought she was too good for me, the little high-flown bitch. She was selling it, and my money's as good as the next man's."

"And later on she was found strangled and raped. After the fight you lay in wait for her, Mefford."

"For Christ's sake." Mefford gave a grunt that was half laugh. "Me? Prove it."

"That's what we aim to do. Where were you when she was killed?"

"Round and about. Drivin' away from the whorehouse. What else?"

"No. You waylaid her."

"Any more fairy stories?"

Charleston turned away from him and said, "Take him back and lock him up, Doolittle. But be careful."

"I just hope he tries something."

"And then bring the woman in."

She came in, a woman showing sharp angles through her ragged outfit, and sat down. Her eyes, red-rimmed, were as sad as a hangover. On one cheek a bruise was fading.

"Do you want an attorney, Mrs. Mefford?" Charleston asked her.

"What for? You got us dead to rights."

"You are Mrs. Mefford?"

"You can call me that. It ain't so, though. My name's Gracie Jones."

"I see. How long have you been living with him?"

"Off and on, quite a while."

"You don't deny hitting my deputy with a frying pan?"

"Ain't his head enough proof?"

"Why did you hit him?"

"Why, for God's sake! Mefford would have kilt me if I hadn't come to help him. He's got a mean streak."

"Why do you go on living with him?"

"What else? What else?" she cried out. "A damn wreck, that's me, wore out and old and no good." She thrust out her knobby hands, showing skinny forearms. "No good for anything else." In her tones was the resignation to total defeat. Of a sudden tears came to her inflamed eyes.

Charleston shifted uneasily. Crying women upset him. After a pause he asked, "Why does he keep you?"

"Ask him. All I know is he doesn't like to cook or tidy up. Maybe that's why. Nothin' else goes on, I can tell you."

"Do you know whether or not he rustled a couple of calves?"

"I wouldn't put it past him, but I don't know. He just brings in meat and tells me to cook it." She had taken a wrinkled handkerchief from her pocket and wiped her eyes. "Half the time I don't know where he is. He just takes off, for an hour or a day or maybe longer."

"You know we're investigating a murder case, the death of that girl near Overthrust?"

"I heerd about it."

"Where was Mefford that night?"

"Don't look up no date and time. I don't know where he was. He don't tell me. Gone, is all."

"What I can't understand, Mrs. Mefford, is why you and he didn't make tracks after you'd left Mr. Beard, here, for dead?"

"You don't know Mefford. I told him we ought to

make ourselves scarce. I told him we were in trouble. But would he move? No. He said no son of a bitch, law or not, was pushing him around. He's balky as a spoiled mule. Not too bright in the head, either. Pretty dumb if you ask me. Crazy dumb."

"But you two get along?"

"Depends on what you mean. We get along fair for a spell, then something happens to roil him and he takes it out on me."

"Beats you up?"

"Plenty. Pret' near kills me."

"And you stand for it?"

"What else?" she said again with old hopelessness in her eyes.

As if he had come to the end of his string, Charleston asked, "I suppose you drive?"

"Don't every civilized person? Sure, bike or trailer, I can drive 'em."

Charleston rose from his chair. "You'll have to appear at the next term of court. It has to be jail until then, unless you make bond."

"Make bond? Put up bail money, and him owin' on the camper and bike. Make bond in a pig's eye."

"Then that's all, I think. Doolittle, will you take Mrs. Mefford back?"

She threw out her work-worn hands. "Please, not in the same cell as Mefford. Separate us. Things goin' against him, and he'll turn on me."

After she had gone, Charleston said, "That's one happy relationship."

8

Two days went by, and nothing happened except for an occasional headache, milder now but still there. I had run out of leads. It did no good to review what little I did know. I said to Charleston, "I'm just a drag. I'll take my turn with the other boys, serving papers, taking calls, whatever comes up. I'm not earning my pay."

"You'll do nothing of the sort," he answered. "You still look peaked. How often do I have to tell you to stay out of the office? Take a week off if need be. That's small pay for the knock on your head."

Without thinking, I put a hand to my temple. The bandage was off. Just a bit of stuck-on gauze remained.

"I'm about to lose hope on this case," I told him.

"That's because you're under par. Keep counting on a break. You never know. Now get out."

I drove out to call on Anita, whose image kept dodging into my mind. She welcomed me and served coffee and cookies. Our talk was friendly enough, and I didn't push, though all the time wanting her in my arms. Our new relationship, I felt sure, was fragile as a spider web. One wrong move, and she would run for a corner.

While we were talking, Omar Test entered. To me he said, "Howdy, Mr. Beard. Hope you are feeling better." He turned to Anita. "I think I'd better go to the north field, Miss Anita, and see how the cows and calves are doing."

She nodded, and he went out the door. Then she said, "I'll be forever indebted to you for finding Omar

for me." It had been a long time since I'd found him,
but it was true that I had. She continued, "Omar may
not be the brightest man in the county, but he's as good
a husbandman as any. He loves animals and likes to see
growing things. So I'm thankful to you." She smiled
into my eyes.

All I could find to say was, "Just be glad it worked
out all right."

That was as close as we came to getting together.

At home I sat in the kitchen while Mother fussed
over supper. Between stirring and forking and looking
into the oven, she said, "I saw old Mr. Ralston today. I
swear I don't know how he makes it to the post office,
old as he is. Must be ninety. He wants to see you,
Jason. He's lonely and out of things. It wouldn't hurt
you to give him a half hour or so. Now would it?"

After supper I set out. It was one of those long
June evenings with the solstice near at hand. In the
west the sun was shooting fire at clouds drifting like
ships. Somewhere a meadowlark sang.

Mr. Ralston lived alone on a side street in a small,
old house with a front porch facing east. He was seated
there in an easy chair, his cane close at hand. As he
tried to get up, I waved him down and shook his
withered hand. His lids drooped over keen eyes. He
hadn't shaved this day, and white bristle stubbled his
cheeks and chin. I imagined shaving was a chore for
him even with electric clippers.

"Sit down, Jase," he said and fell silent in the
manner of old-timers whose present is mixed with the
past.

"I'm back in the sheriff's office," I told him.

He nodded and after another pause, just remembering, said, "We used to call the likes of you heel flies.
That was a while ago. Had 'em on my heels for that
matter."

Into the silence I said, "I brought a bottle."

He thought about it and asked, "Bourbon?"

"That's it."

"Smart to remember. Reckon you can find glasses and the water tap inside. Or I can do it."

"No. No. I'll make out."

I heard him say as I made for the kitchen, "Can't stomach Scotch. Musty straw stack."

The kitchen was pretty tidy, considering. I found glasses and the water faucet, poured drinks and returned.

"I'll bet they never caught you," I said, not as a question. Ask an old Westerner a direct question and you shut him up. We drank.

"Oh, heel flies. Twice they buzzed after me, and me not to blame much either time. With a good horse I outfooted 'em."

He sat, probably thinking about those times, and I brought him up by saying, "This heel fly, me, I'm after the man who killed the girl at Overthrust."

"Seems I heard something about that. Chippie, wasn't she?"

"That's right."

He took more whiskey into his mouth and savored the flavor. "Making any headway?"

"Not much." I sipped. "Sometimes I think it was a young man, sometimes an older one."

"No tally there."

"Nope."

He emptied his glass, and I refilled it, thinking a couple of drinks would get him to say more. It did.

"Two kinds to think on," he said. "Young pups and old dogs."

"Takes in all men."

I might not have spoken. He went on, "Young pups don't have training. Old dogs want to bust out of it. Take a young pup and give him a couple of beers, and he's hell on wheels, or thinks so. Busts things up and calls it fun. The worst ones got rape in their pants and maybe murder in their fool hands. Not too many of them, but still too many."

I said, "I savvy the pups better than the old dogs."

He took a sip, saying, "I can't stand this stuff like I used to." Then he went on, "Comes a time in a man's life, say fifty or so, when he feels the sand slippin' out from under him, so he tries to turn and get a fresh foothold. It riles him when he can't make it. It riles him when a woman ain't willin', the old fool."

Having spoken, he lifted his glass.

The silence was broken by a car full of young people who raced by, radio at full blast, voices screaming.

The old man followed them with his eyes and his ears, and with silence restored said, "Pussy and pecker, that's all they think about."

"Always been that way."

"No, sir. That's where you're wrong." The liquor had given him greater voice. "Sure, those things entered in, but they weren't the whole ticket."

"No?"

"We had a whole world to roam in, a whole world to think in. Why, my uncle rode horseback from his ranch to the Falls to hear William Jennings Bryan, him that thought to be president. That's fifty miles or more, and not a gate to open the whole way." Mr. Ralston chucked a phlegmy chuckle. "Charles Russell now, the painter you know, he wouldn't go. He called Bryan a windjammer like he would other politicians. Had a great sense of humor. Once he said he'd like to meet the son of a bitch that called dried apples fruit." He chuckled again. "Not many own to it, but I say Russell was a better man than he was painter, which ain't casting off on his pictures."

I wanted him back on track and said, "A whole world to roam in."

"I traveled many a mile by horse," he said, the older days in his voice. "Yep, a whole world. A whole world to dream in."

"So?"

"Some of them come true, just some of them. That didn't matter. What mattered was dreamin'."

I left him, dreaming what dreams he still might have, leaving the remains of the bottle.

*   *   *

I had nothing to do the next morning and felt like doing just that, what with a low ache in my head. So I got out of bed late, had breakfast with Mother and wandered downtown. I went into the Bar Star, had a small beer and small talk with Bob Studebaker, who wanted to know how my case was going.

"Nowhere," I told him.

From there I stepped to the bank to transfer my small out-of-town balance. Mike Day was as effusive as ever. "I want you to see something, Jase," he said and led me to a room in the back. Young Roland Day sat there, looking gnomish with his dark glasses and phones plugged in his ears. Beside him were a record player in operation and a tape machine. I supposed he was taping records.

"Regular nut on this stuff," Mike Day said, soft-voiced for once. "He's right here when he's not needed up front. Got lots of equipment, you can see. Got a good idea, too. Come the holidays or Easter or some other occasion, we'll flood the building with sweet music. We'll make it festive and appropriate, choosing our own tunes, not depending on canned stuff. How about it?"

I told him it seemed like a good idea.

Out of habit I went to the office and found Charleston frowning, not yet seated. His first words were, "How you feeling, Jase? No headaches?"

"Not to speak of."

"That means you have. Why don't you keep out of my sight, as directed?"

"I have to be somewhere. Anything new?"

He strode to his chair, slammed into it and blew out a breath. "Yes, damn and pisswillie. The dirty birds have flown."

"You don't mean—"

"But I do. My mistake. I asked for a low bond for Mefford and the woman. They didn't have a slim dime between them. But it turned out he had a brother in the city who was doing all right. He sprang them."

"Ease off. You couldn't have known."

"Dumb, just the same. They made tracks, I suppose for Chicken Coulee. Maybe afoot. Maybe the brother drove them. I don't know. Anyhow, they're out."

"They'll have to appear in court later."

"And do what in the meantime?" He shrugged his shoulders. "At any rate I don't think they'll try to skedaddle, not with his brother as bondsman."

"They wouldn't get far in that old camper and those worn-out tires. One of them at least is flat."

"So I noticed."

I should have known he would.

"We'll wait, Jase. They say murder will out, and this one will. We'll watch and wait."

9

The phone rang. I flipped on a night light and saw hazily it was sometime after midnight. I rolled out of bed, hoping Mother hadn't wakened.

"Emergency, Jase," the voice on the phone said. It was Blanche Burton speaking. It took me a second to recognize that. "Report to the office at once." She hung up.

I hurried into my clothes. Mother was at the bedroom door, a housecoat over her nightie. "What, Jase?"

"Emergency. That's all I know."

Her "Please be careful" followed me out the door.

Blanche Burton at the board thumbed the way to the inner office. "They're all in there except Halvor."

"What's up?"

"You'll find out."

Cole, Doolittle and Charleston were in the office, all standing. Amussen came in right after me.

Charleston, erect behind his desk, told us, "Here's what I have. The Stuart girl is missing."

Doolittle asked, "The singer?"

"The singer. Her father called me. That was less than half an hour ago." He looked at his watch. "One o'clock now. He had telephoned all her friends. No help there. He walked the road twice, from school to home. He found nothing. I sent him back to the house."

Amussen broke in, "She's just a kid, and you know what kids are. Joy-riding or something."

"Not this girl."

49

"Wait," I said. "She had voice practice tonight, or last night it is now?"

"Right. I meant to tell you. It was over at ten o'clock, after dark." He went on, "She always ran home after practice. That was part of her fitness program, to develop lung power. She always arrived on time. Quarter of a mile from school to home, the way unlighted."

Charleston looked us over. "All right. We look for her this way. We'll travel the sides of the road, about twenty yards apart. If we find nothing, we broaden the search. Understand?"

Amussen said, "Damn few for a search party."

"I'll call in others if need be. The town marshal. State police. It's up to us right now. Any better ideas?"

"Who was at practice?" I asked.

"In good time, Jase. Don't jump the gun. I have flashlights for all of you, and whistles. Two blasts if you find anything. Come on."

We drove to the high school in two cars and deployed there, Charleston, Cole and Amussen taking the broader side of the road, Doolittle and I the other. I took a position outside his.

With a full moon overhead, we hardly had need of the flashlights, using them only for what the moon didn't reveal—shadows behind clumps of grass, pockets of darkness in uneven land. I heard Doolittle muttering to himself. I heard the silence of night, broken by the far-off cry of a coyote. In such a singing, moon-flooded night, nothing much could be wrong, I told myself.

Two whistle blasts broke the quiet. I ran toward the sound. False alarm. Amussen, finding an old and discarded overcoat, had whistled before he looked close. It was an ancient garment, blown there by the wind or cast off by who knew whom, and grass had sprouted through the holes in it.

In twenty minutes or so we arrived almost together at the Stuart premises. I glimpsed a lone, shadowed figure standing on the porch. Charleston called to it, "Nothing, Mr. Stuart. We'll keep looking." Seeing that lonely, hopeful, anxious man, I was glad I wasn't a father.

We turned and started back, moving out farther from the road.

It was my luck to find her. I slipped going down a narrow, little gully in which a few willows sprouted. I threw down a hand to save a fall. The hand felt something. It felt cloth.

I turned on the flash. Half-hidden by the brush, there was a body. I made myself look closer. It was nightmare time, the once-pretty face, swollen and suffused, looking open-eyed and open-mouthed at me. I forced out a hand and found a wrist, though I knew there was no need. I pulled the skirt down over blood. Then I stepped up the bank and sat down.

All the blind evil of the world was concentrated there in the gully, all the random injustice. They were there and they bore me down. The bright promise snuffed out, the hopes, the dreams, the good, gay manner all for nothing, the spirit dead and the young body.

What was the use of vengeance against the all-evil? What was justice, loved by officers and the law, when such injustice existed? The tormented face swam in my mind.

Then I thought to blow the whistle.

Doolittle reached me first and asked where. He took a look and said, "Suffering Jesus!" He came back and put a hand on my shoulder. "Tough, Jase. Knocks a man out. Take it easy."

The others arrived, Charleston in the lead. I sat where I was. He stepped down the bank, looked and returned. He was saying through his teeth, "Son of a bitch. Son of a bitch." The words were fit, even for a man who disliked vulgarity.

His voice rose. "Stand back! Stand back, all of you. We'll go over the ground in the morning." He played his flashlight down and up. "Don't see any drag marks." Then, "Cole, any chance of pictures tonight?"

"No trouble."

"Get your equipment here then. Doolittle, notify Doc Yak and Underwood. Amussen, you stay here until relieved." He shook his head. "I have to tell Mr. Stuart. Rather be hanged."

Perhaps because I was seated and silent, he seemed not to notice me until then. His flash shone in my face. "You stay with me, Jase. Things to do."

"There's nothing anybody can do."

"Don't be foolish."

"I'm going home."

His voice came out sharp. "Going home? Go, then."

"Yes, sir." I got up.

Before I left his tone softened. "See you in the morning, Jason. For now, just forget if you can."

10

The lights were on in the house, and Mother was waiting for me when I got home. "An ungodly hour to be up and dressed," I told her.

"Oh, Jase, I'm glad you're home and home safe." She looked into my face, and her eyes widened. "Something's wrong. Something dreadful."

"Yes."

"Don't tell me about it yet. You need food. You look so drawn. I'll fix an omelette." She was acting in character. Food for me first of all.

"I'm not hungry. Any whiskey in the house?"

She began cracking eggs. "I believe there's some medical spirits in the far cabinet."

That, I thought, was what I needed. Medicine and spirit. I found the bottle, poured three fingers and added water. Then I sat down.

"Some food will do you good."

"Don't hurry. Let the medicine take effect." I took a long swallow from the glass, then another. Almost at once I felt the warmth of the alcohol, for whatever good it did me.

In short order she served the omelette with toast and put the coffee pot on. I pecked at the food. She waited for me to speak.

"I'm not cut out for this work," I told her.

She regarded me with astonishment. "Whatever makes you say that?"

"I found a young girl violated and choked to death."

"Someone you know?"

"Just in passing. It was the Stuart girl. Virginia Stuart."

"God in heaven, Jase!"

"I doubt it."

"The little singer killed! What will the Stuarts do? How can they stand it? They were so proud of her. Who, Jase? Who was the monster?"

"No idea." I rose and poured another drink, lighter this time.

"You have to find him."

"Why?"

"You know why. For justice. So he won't do it again."

"Let somebody else find him."

She took a deep breath, and her words came out in a gush. "For the first time in my life I'm glad your father isn't alive to hear you."

"You didn't see her."

She sat down at the table and gazed at me, her eyes earnest and pleading. "Jason, dear son, you're so beaten, but you won't give up. You've spent a good many years with Sheriff Charleston, a good many in school, believing in a career as an officer. I never wanted you to go into law enforcement. That was selfish. I was afraid for you. But you insisted, and I accepted. You wanted to make the world a safe place to live in. I'm sure you still do. You won't let yourself down."

I put my hand over hers, feeling the rough grain of a hand that had worked too long and too hard. "I've seen dead people before, a good many, but never one like this."

"Of course it turned your stomach."

"Turned my mind is more like it."

"For the time being. That's all."

"I don't know, Mother. I'm going to bed."

She rose as I did, put her arms around me and patted my shoulder, saying, "There. There." With twenty-odd years knocked off, she would have been singing about Winken, Blinken, and Nod.

If I slept at all that night, it was a tortured sleep. The ravaged face, the torn body, were there before me, under the smiling moon. She was there before and after, the pretty, polite schoolgirl and the later horror. I got out of bed at dawn. The bright banners of the sun shone in the east, and the cheerful sun itself was just edging up. I yanked the blind down. Not sleeping, I made myself lie still.

I lagged to the office in the morning, feeling half dead and out of the world. Cole was on the board, yawning. "Never a dull moment." he said.

"Morning, Jase," Charleston said from his desk. "Mr. Stuart is due any minute. He insisted on coming, saying his wife couldn't stand any questions. Doolittle and Amussen are finding out who attended the practice session last night. Some will come in willingly. We'll visit those who can't conveniently appear. If any refuse we'll see about subpoenas."

For lack of something better, I said, "Wheels in motion."

"What about Mefford?"

"In good time, Jase. In good time. He's back at the camper. Old Mr. Gates called in to tell me so."

"Gates?"

"You remember. The man with the missing calves. He lives pretty close to Mefford."

"Yes. I'm scheduling interviews for tomorrow, thinking the funeral will probably be the next day. We're too pushed for sessions today, too pushed and, more than that, too dull, too devilish drowsy for good thinking. In addition, there's a county commissioners' meeting this afternoon. It's important I show up. Anyhow, glad you're here. You'll take notes, of course."

"If you want me to."

Mr. Stuart came in then. He was a small, erect man, dressed in a tweed three-piece suit. He wore a trim Van Dyke and put me in mind of an old-world judge. At Charleston's invitation he sat down stiffly.

"A miserable business, I know, Mr. Stuart," Charleston told him. "I can't regret it as much as you, but I do regret it."

Stuart didn't answer. The knuckles of his hands turned white from his grip on the chair arms. There was violence in him, I thought, and a rage that burned under stern control. And, with them, in his eyes was a sorrow that it hurt to see.

"I'll try to make things short," Charleston said. "Just a few details I need to know. Your daughter's name was Virginia Stuart?"

"Aye."

"I know you've identified her."

"Aye." The beard moved to the tightening of his jaw muscles. "What was left."

"Her age?"

"Just sixteen."

"She was accustomed to running home after practice?"

"Every time." I caught the Scottish burr in his speech. He put a handkerchief to his lips. "We never had reason to chide her."

"That's what I've gathered. Is there anything, any reason to suspect anybody?"

"There must be reasons, but I know of none."

"She was popular with her classmates?"

"With everyone, I think. She enjoyed people of her own age but never was serious about a boy, if you're driving at that. She planned a career."

"I'm not driving at anything especially, Mr. Stuart. Just asking questions. How long have you lived in the county?"

"Four years."

"And what brought you here?"

"My wife's health. She is far from well—and worse now."

"And where did you live before?"

"What does it matter, Mr. Charleston? All this is not to the point."

"Probably not. But sometimes background helps. Please bear with me."

"Since you ask, we had a home in Cincinnati in Ohio river country. I was an accountant. The climate affected my wife adversely. We moved here."

"Just the one child, the gifted child?"

"Aye." The word "gifted" seemed to spark Stuart. "With the one we were blessed. We had such hopes, such ambitions for her." Control failed him for an instant, and he shook his head to restore it. He put his handkerchief to his eyes and returned it to his pocket. "I am not a wealthy man, Mr. Charleston, and I dislike charity. But when the town started a collection for her musical career, how could I refuse? The money was not for charity. It was for a cause, for the sake of a rare gift, for art. I accepted."

"Of course," Charleston answered. "I would have done the same."

"Is that all, Mr. Charleston?"

"I think so. Thank you."

Now Stuart jerked forward, his face outthrust. "Catch the goddomned mon!" His voice was rough with rage, and I thought I felt the once-held rage emanating from his clothes. "Aye. Catch him and I'll kill him."

"When we catch him, the law will take care of him," Charleston said in even tones.

Stuart left the office, walking erect, his violence contained.

Once he was gone, Charleston said, "Well, Jase?" When I didn't answer, he asked, "What do you think?"

"I'm not sure I'm thinking."

He gave me a long appraisal, then went on quietly, "You remember that Doolittle once thought the law was too cruel and threatened to resign? I believe it was you who talked him out of it." He wanted me to say yes, but I kept silent. "Well, sure enough, the law works cruelly sometimes. Sometimes it works against itself. But in spite of its cruelty, in spite of its miscues, the law is necessary. It is about all we have, more important than any religion, any isms, for a livable society. Think on that."

I was saved an answer by the entrance of Doc Yak.

He slammed into the office without waiting to be announced. "Simple job," he burst out without seating himself. "Simple, goddamn, beastly job." He threw an envelope on the desk. "There's the report."

"Sit down and ease the pressure."

"There's more sons of bitches in this world than all the wonders of heaven and hell," he said, throwing himself into a chair. He glared at us in turn. "You've got a madman on your hands. Two girls dead, raped and strangled. What next?"

"Next we catch him—or them," Charleston answered evenly.

"Yeah, spread your butterfly net."

"Tell us what you found."

"It's in the report, but what do you think I'm here for, to play pinochle?"

"Proceed, Doc."

"The subject was in excellent health. Female. Age fifteen or so. A virgin deflowered by violence. The bastard who did it had big hands."

"Anything more?"

"What in hell do you mean, anything more? Want her drawn and quartered?"

"Calm down, Doc. Time of death?"

"Ten or eleven o'clock, more or less either way. That satisfy you?"

"She left the school at ten P.M. to run home. That shouldn't take more than fifteen minutes at the outside. Your time fits. Thanks."

But Doc wasn't through. He pushed his beaked face farther out of the shell of shirt and coat and said, "So you go about this all methodical, using up time, interviewing everyone and his uncle, and the bastard runs free."

"Doc," Charleston said with an edge in his voice, "tell me a better way or shut up."

Doc drew in his head. "Hell, Chick, I know it's a hell's scramble. Don't take offense."

Charleston drew a hand across his brow. "All right."

After he had gone, Charleston told me, "Take off,

Jase. Get the hell out. Try for some sleep. We're all dead on our feet. I'll send Doolittle and Amussen home when they report. Get Cole relief, too. Blanche Burton likes overtime. Go."

I had time to say, "You're as tired as anybody."

"Never mind. Make tracks."

I followed orders but didn't go home. I drove out to Anita's. Around the barnyard as I approached, chickens and turkeys were feeding, the hens with strings and circles of young ones close by, some shedding their down, others new-hatched. Omar Test stood in the middle of them, looking cheerful, moving slow. He waved a welcoming hand. At another time I would have found the scene pleasing.

"Why, Jase," Anita said at the door. "Come on in. Happy to see you."

I sat and she sat at the kitchen table. "Looks like you have poultry," I said for lack of something better.

"Omar's so good with them."

For the moment I had nothing more to say. I just looked at her, at the fair hair, the blooming cheeks, the generous mouth now forming a question. "What's wrong?"

"Haven't you heard?"

"No. Not today, I've been busy."

"Everything's wrong."

"Do I have to guess?"

"I'm losing my taste for law enforcement."

"That's news. Why?"

"Last night I found a young girl. She'd been raped and killed, choked to death first maybe."

"Who was it?"

"Her name's Virginia Stuart."

"I know of her. She sings, doesn't she?"

"She did. And you must be careful. That's two girls strangled and violated. Extra careful. Who knows?"

She considered, watching my face. "So you've lost your enthusiasm?"

"You didn't see her."

"But you did, and it's numbed you."

"That's hardly the word. It was too much for me.

It's still too much. I see that face all the time. I see the blood. I should have studied business or art or something."

She put a hand out and held mine. "One time, to me, you spoke out for law enforcement as your choice of a career. You were pretty hot. You said it was as important as the raising of food."

"But you didn't believe me."

"I've a lot to be forgiven for, Jase."

"Forget it. I'm coming to believe you were right."

"Jase." She leaned forward, her small chin thrust out. "I wouldn't give a nickel for the man who wasn't hurt, shocked and repelled by what you saw. He would be cold, inhuman, capable of murder himself."

"You can say that again."

Now her words grew more intense. "But I would expect the strong man to shake off his paralysis and do what had to be done."

"Nice phrase, paralysis of horror."

She released my hand. "Have I been too blunt?"

"Blunt enough."

"But you're strong."

"Thanks. Time will tell." I got up, said goodbye and left her, not looking back. I had heard lectures enough for today.

11

Charleston and I arrived at the courthouse door together. It was eight A.M., too early for the other county workers to be stirring.

A man was waiting in the outer office. Amussen at the board said, "A gent here to see you." The man rose and took off his hat, revealing a head of thick, white hair. He said to us, "I am B. A. Antonelli." He was dressed in tailored gray, a white shirt, and blue tie. His black shoes glistened. A white mustache contrasted with a complexion darker than that of most of us. I took him to be in his early seventies, though his eyes appeared young and eloquent.

"As soon as I heard," he went on, "I came. You want to talk to me. Yes?"

"I do. You were Virginia's voice teacher. Am I right?"

"Her coach. Yes."

Charleston led us into the inner office and asked Antonelli to take a chair. Antonelli sat down easily, quickly, and, I thought, exactly. I made ready with pencil and notebook.

"You received our message, then?" Charleston said.

"Message? No. I heard by the radio, so I came. It is a great tragedy."

Charleston nodded gravely.

"A tragedy to be taken so young, at the very promise of life. But greater still because of the voice."

"It was unusual, I understand."

"Unusual? That is too mild. I have heard the great

61

ones. I heard Lily Pons at her greatest. Our little girl would have been better still." His brown eyes, full of pain, looked us over. "My friends, how can words say?" His delicate hands spread in a little gesture that in itself spoke grief and loss.

I was taken back to my college days and a paragraph written by the philosopher Alfred North Whitehead. He had said something about style, citing it as the ultimate morality of man. Style, not stylishness. Style in the sense of skill and economy in action, in attaining ends.

Charleston was saying, "How did you happen to be teaching, coaching her?"

"That is left to me at the least, helping young singers. Once I had a good voice, not great but good, and I have had small parts in operas. Also I play the violin and have played it professionally, in house orchestras and at concerts given at this place and that. I bore you, sir?"

"Not at all. Please go on."

"With age the voice falters. It loses range and timbre and vibrancy. And the hands themselves are not so skillful with the strings."

"I see."

"But I have retained the keen ear, the gift of true pitch. That, I thought, was not enough. So when my son, a doctor, moved with his family to Montana, I followed him, thinking to retire. But there were young voices to help, young singers to train. So not quite retirement for me. Last fall your school heard of me, and I came."

"And were training Virginia?"

"Just a little help maybe. As much as I could. With breathing, with exercises, with postures, only a bit here and there, and always the encouragement. She needed to go to the finest of schools." He took an instant's pause. "You know, with the help of Mr. Mike Day, we were collecting a fund for her schooling?"

"I believe everyone with a loose dollar contributed to it."

"Yes. Such a small thing, she was, and her voice big and true and distinctive. Hearing her, you thought how the wren was too small for its voice, the lark too small, but there was the music. Such a future she had! I could hear her in America, in Europe, with the best companies. And everywhere she sang to acclaim. And now all ashes. All silence." Again he made that little gesture of nothingness.

"Tell me about that last practice," Charleston asked, "who was there?"

"Not many. But I am not acquainted. The principal, yes, in and out. A boy of red hair called Pat. A few others. I do not know names."

The buzzer on Charleston's desk sounded. Charleston wasn't pleased. "What is it?"

I could hear Amussen's voice. "The Bar Star was broken into last night and a lot of booze taken."

"So? We'll get to that."

"But Bob Studebaker's here in the office, yelling for action."

"Tell him I'll see him at noon, not before then. Hear?"

That done, Charleston turned again to Antonelli. "When practice was over, what did you do?"

"So I am a suspect. Yes?" An instant's smile showed under the mustache. "You are right. Suspect all until you know for a certainty. I drove back to the city at once."

Charleston fiddled with a pencil, then raised his eyes. "I would put you last on my list of suspects, Mr. Antonelli. I doubt I would list you at all."

"Thank you. It is not good to be suspected. It is a shock. It would be to me an offense in this case, but you have not offended."

"Then I think that's all."

"One thing more, please. If I can assist, even a little, I will cancel everything and stay here."

"I'll let you know. Thanks for coming."

As soon as he had gone, Charleston turned to me and said, "Best of the old world."

I spoke without interest, "Going after Mefford?"

"I'm making sure he stays put. Flew over the camper with Al Watson while you were absent and saw him."

"Well?"

"I'm keeping him in reserve."

I said, "I see," though I didn't.

"He doesn't fit, not to me, and grilling him would be useless without something to go on."

"He killed one girl."

"So we think, though without proof. But the second girl? I don't believe it."

I let out a tired sigh. "All right with me. Let him go."

He answered with a sharp, "Pisswillie," and might have said more but Amussen buzzed to announce, "There's a kid waiting."

"Send him in."

A red-headed, freckled boy entered, seeming a trifle abashed but not overly so. He was maybe sixteen.

"Sit down, son," Charleston told him mildly. "You may be able to help us. You attended Virginia Stuart's last practice?"

"Yes, sir. Sure did."

"And your name is Pat Lenihan?"

"That's me all right. I liked to hear her sing."

"And you liked her, too. Didn't you have a date or two with her?"

"More'n that but not much. Why?"

"I'm just poking around."

The boy smiled. "No need to poke at me. Holy cow, I wouldn't have killed her, not for anything."

"You were stuck on her, I take it."

The kid wriggled, and a flush came on his freckled face. "Well, all right. Sure. I was gone on her. Anything wrong with that?"

"Not a thing."

"To tell the truth, I wanted her to go steady with me, but she wasn't about to go steady with anybody. No, sir. Her singing was what mattered."

"What did you do when practice was over?"

"I went straight home. My old man's strict."

"Do you have any reason to suspect anyone you saw at that practice?"

"Why, no. Not a soul. Who would touch a hair of her head?"

"Somebody did."

The boy bent his head and sat silent for a minute. When he lifted his eyes, I saw tears in them. "Why, Mr. Charleston?" he cried out. "Tell me why? It's such a goddamn shame."

"It is that, son." Charleston let him go.

The principal, Alfred Parsons, was next. "I know you announced you would drop around to see me, but I had a free period and so am saving you the trouble."

Charleston thanked him. Nothing that Parsons saw, heard or suspected helped us along.

It was almost noon when he closed the door behind him. I said what was first in my mind. "When are you tackling Mefford?"

"We'll get to him. He's still at the camper. Mr. Gates is watching and will report if Mefford tries to take off. Satisfied?"

"No, sir."

"I'm playing a hunch with some reason behind it. Just let it be for the present."

We called a halt then and set out for the Bar Star. Every doorway along the street held a questioner. Others tried to stop us as we walked. Some of them were sorry or horrified, some were vengeful, some merely curious. Charleston tried to be patient, brushing them off as easily as he could.

The Bar Star was full. There is nothing like shocking news to send men to the bottle. We shook our heads to questions again. Bob Studebaker hustled from behind the bar, telling his helper to take over. Outrage had flushed his face. "'Bout time you showed up," he told Charleston.

"Tell us about it."

"Last night after closing some bastard broke in the

back window and made off with almost a case of good whiskey. Not bar stuff. I. W. Harper, Old Forrester, and the like of that."

"Cash?"

"Just whiskey. Nothing else."

"Have you notified the town police?"

"Sure, but Christ Almighty! You know what they're like. Fair at traffic, good at seeing business doors are locked at night, extra good at seeing the bars close on time. That's it, though. Give 'em an honest-to-God crime, and they mess their pants."

We had become the center of a little crowd, all silent, all listening.

"All right. I'll put Amussen on it."

Studebaker drew his stomach into his chest in order to blow harder. "Now lookee here. I'm asking for your best. Not that horse."

Charleston answered with the even voice that showed irritation, "We have a murder on our hands. Not one. Two."

"Goddamnit, this is my place. I pay taxes. It's my whiskey stolen. I want results. And I don't want Amussen."

"Studebaker, you'll take what we can give you. We'll give you Amussen. It's his kind of case. Just be grateful."

Before we turned away, Studebaker said, "Aw, shit, Chick. Pardon me all to hell. I'm awful agitated."

We had a beer and then lunch at the Jackson Hotel.

Once outside it, Charleston said, "Let's drop in the bank. I want to talk to Mike Day, and you see if you can't cut young Day out of the crowd and quiz him a little."

Mike Day was announcing to customers who came and went or idled, "The bank is offering a ten-thousand-dollar reward. Yes, ten thousand dollars goes to the man who turns up the murderer. I want everyone to know that."

Charleston managed to get Day aside. I motioned to young Day, who was bent over papers at his desk beyond an open counter. He got to his feet, and I thumbed in the direction of the back room where he kept his musical equipment. We stood as we talked. I started out by asking, "Have you any idea, any at all, about Virginia's killer?"

"I can't imagine. I just can't imagine."

"You were fond of her, weren't you?"

"Wasn't everybody?"

"Not as you were. How were you making out?"

Behind his dark glasses his eyes flickered, like light blue under running water. "I don't have to answer such personal questions."

"That's a fact. But will you?"

"Don't you see it's personal. Can't you see it's painful?"

"So is rape and murder."

"Horrible," he said. "Just horrible." I would have thought his face paled if it wasn't by nature pale.

"I asked you how you were making out with her."

"We were friends."

"More than that. You wanted to have her."

"I wanted her to be my wife."

"Meantime, were you intimate? Sexually, that is?"

His answer came in little explosions. "No. No. She wasn't that kind of a girl."

"But when she wouldn't let you, I imagine you got mad?"

"Think what you want to, but I couldn't get mad at her. Disappointed is what I was."

I couldn't read anything in that white face or see anything in those shielded eyes. He had his hands clasped in front of him. They were big hands. So were mine.

I repeated his words. "She wasn't that kind of a girl?"

"That's what I said."

"How can you be so sure? She had other dates."

His body tightened now. He said through thin lips, "That's an insult. A slur on her memory. Goodbye."

I shook my head. "Sorry then." I tried to see his eyes. "You think a man could get to her only by force?"

"I know it. I know it. As I told you, I wanted to marry her. We were both interested in music, and I was sure we could get along."

"She wasn't of age."

"I was willing to wait. I told her that."

"She refused?"

"Yes, she refused." All of a sudden he slumped, put his hands over his eyes and bowed his head. Then he raised a tear-stained face. His voice came out in a cry. "Sure she refused. Who wouldn't, goddamnit! Marry a poor son of a bitch of a ghost with weak eyes! Who wants that? What can an albino hope for? Not one goddamn thing. I hate God."

I put a hand on his shoulder, feeling sympathy for him and shame for myself. "All right, Roland. All right."

We joined, Charleston and I, outside the bank and, walking to the office, exchanged useless information.

The afternoon produced nothing helpful. The school music teacher showed up. So did more kids. So did old man Shirley Southby, who thought he had written an opera with a big part in it for Virginia Stuart. They exhausted the list of those present at the last practice.

At six o'clock, as Charleston stretched, I said, "I'm going home, get a quick supper, and come back to type all this dreary stuff."

"It could wait until tomorrow."

"I want to get it off my hands. It's no good. Not one clue, not one helpful idea, in the lot. But, then, I didn't expect any."

Charleston looked at me, not smiling, and answered, "Never expect anything, Jase, and you'll never be disappointed—and probably never surprised."

I told him, "Thanks."

12

The whole force, except for Blanche Burton, attended Virginia Stuart's funeral, though not in one group. I had to accompany Mother, who dressed in black, wore a hat and pulled on long black gloves. For all formal occasions and some not so formal, she wore gloves as if, without them, she would be baring something better left covered.

The service took place in the Methodist church, which couldn't accommodate all those who came. Quite a number stood outside in pleasant sunshine. With the church windows open they could hear most of what went on.

As Mother and I were ushered to seats, I caught a glimpse of Mr. and Mrs. Stuart. A small woman, dressed in mourning, she wore a long overcoat, too heavy for anyone save an invalid. A dark scarf covered half her face. I was put in mind of something coming out of a cocoon. Mr. Stuart sat straight, rigid as angle iron. Near them was Mr. Antonelli, looking sad.

The coffin, covered, rested on a platform just below the pulpit. To one side of the pulpit stood the high school mixed quartet. To the wheezy chords of the organ the long-coated minister came forward and read from the Bible.

"The righteous live forever, and the care of them is with the Most High; with His right hand shall He cover them, and with His arm shall He shield them."

He bowed his head and began a prayer, "Mighty God, fount of all life . . ."

His words droned on, lost in my self-concern, lost

69

in my thoughts of the abused and dead girl in the gulley and of my sick horror. As a consequence of that image and my reaction I had been short with Mother, almost quarreled with Anita and been less than courteous to Chick Charleston, my best friend.

The school quartet sang "Beautiful Isle of Somewhere." It was meant, I supposed, to be heartening. The teacher must have put the singers through an intensive drill, for their performance wasn't too ragged.

I had to get hold of myself, I said silently. I had to find in myself what I wanted to do. If law enforcement, or aspects of it, repelled me, then what? No purpose in thinking, though. Just sit and be miserable.

The minister was reading again. "Eternal God, Who committest to us the swift and solemn trust of life . . ."

All the gods of all the faiths couldn't undo what had been done. What consolation in the thought that Virginia might already be singing in the heavenly choir?

The minister looked away from his Bible and said on his own, "A loved one has been taken away from us for reasons no mortal can understand. The Lord works in mysterious ways for His own purposes. But let us have faith in the divine wisdom. And may the good Lord extend to the sorrowing the healing power of His love."

There followed the Lord's Prayer, recited by preacher and audience, and his final words, "The grace of the Lord Jesus Christ, and the love of God, and the communion of the Holy Spirit, be with you all."

Most of those present joined in the parade to the cemetery, where the quartet sang "Abide with Me." On the bare and breezy hillside, against the great silence of the high plains, their voices rose frail and sad and were blown away. The minister went through his final ritual. I thought I could hear the clump of sod on the casket as Mother and I drove away.

She said as we poked along in the car, "Mr. Stuart, I'm sure, is a Presbyterian. I wonder how he felt about John Wesley?"

"In the absence of a Presbyterian church, he had

no choice. Are Calvin and Wesley so different then?" I asked. "Anyhow, it's over."

I left her at home and went to the office. Ralph Otter, the reporter and ad-hustler for the local *Messenger*, was waiting, along with an older man. Otter introduced him as Sam Worthington, special correspondent from the city. "We hope to have a word with Sheriff Charleston," Worthington said. In almost the same instant Charleston entered. With him were Doolittle, Cole and Amussen. He told the two reporters to come into the inner office. I didn't know whether he wanted me there, but I went.

Once we were seated, Worthington said, "I hope you have some frésh copy for us, sheriff."

"Nothing much to add to what I told you previously. When were you in here?"

"Just yesterday, no, day before. I caught you alone. Remember?"

"Vaguely. Since then we've questioned everyone who attended the girl's final practice and a few others in addition."

"And?"

"Nothing on the surface. We have to go through the statements again. And then, maybe, again."

"That's not much to hang a story on."

"That's all there is."

"No fresh or new directions?"

"Just more questions. Further search."

"Two murders and no clues, huh?"

Charleston's tone was sharp. "We're not filing the cases away."

Worthington shook his head. Otter kept quiet as if in the presence of greater talent. "The murders were much alike. Violent, death and rape. Do you suspect just one man?"

"Not necessarily."

"Two, then, one in imitation of the other, a copy-cat crime."

"Can you imagine we haven't thought of that?"

"Or perhaps just one man? After one killing others come easier, so they say."

"I should add you to the force."

When Worthington stood up, Charleston continued, "You may say we're going to catch the man or men."

"How can you be sure of that?"

"Consult our record, Mr. Worthington."

To the closing door Charleston said, "Smart people, these newspapermen."

Doolittle rapped and came in. "Anything for me?"

"Not now. How about lunch?"

I wasn't hungry and so shook my head. Doolittle said he would eat later. "Hold the fort then," Charleston told us and left the room.

Doolittle sat down and grinned at me. "Jase, pardon me all to hell, but every time I look at you a piece of a poem runs in my mind. Like this: 'I am weary of days and hours, blown buds of barren flowers.' You're the barren flower, my friend, dead on the stem."

"What of it?"

"Exercise is what of it. A good workout."

"Is that so, doctor?"

"Yep. I prescribe two or three rounds to work the poison out."

"You're against me, with gloves?"

"Sure. I got it set up."

"David and Goliath, for God's sake. I outweigh you what? Forty pounds?"

"Never mind that. It's the boxer against the puncher. Sometimes I feel sorry for poor old Goliath. Poor bastard didn't have a friend on earth and none to help him. Next thing, if you're game, I'm going to feel sorry for you." He kept grinning at me, a question in his eyes.

I said, "This is crazy."

"I got it set up with that Lenihan kid. There's gloves at the high school and a kind of a ring. I bought trunks for both of us, and here's a stopwatch for the rounds."

"I can't punch you around. Not fair."

"You're right you can't punch me around. The question is will you try?"

"You acted pretty damn sure I would. And you're mighty sure of yourself."

The whole idea was foolish, but I could use some exercise, and I'd pull my punches. I said, "It's dumb, but all right."

At the switchboard Doolittle said, "King, we'll be at the high school for an hour or less. Anyone asks, tell them we're pursuing our investigation, besides tuning up for the final push."

We walked to the high school. Pat Lenihan met us at the door, a wondering eagerness in his eyes. With classes in summer recess, no one else was about.

"All set, kid?" Doolittle asked.

"Sure am. Follow me." He led us into the gymnasium. There was a ring of sorts in it. "Our phys-ed instructor believed in what he called the manly art of self-defense, but the parents objected to black eyes and headaches, so he got fired."

Young Lenihan showed us the locker room, where we peeled off our clothes and put on trunks. "I figured we could do without shoes," Doolittle told me. "Want to punch the bag a little, or jump rope?"

"No need to."

We walked back to the ring.

"All right, kid," Doolittle said. "Come and put the gloves on us. Here's the stopwatch. Three two-minute rounds with a minute between. Understand?"

We climbed into the ring, each in his own corner. After a second or two the kid rang the bell. We came from our corners, ready, and Doolittle landed a light left on my eye. It was a powder-puff punch, and I told myself to go easy. I tried a left and right, missing both. Dancing in, Doolittle tapped me again. He was fast on his feet and fast with his hands. He flitted around me, shifting, dodging, ducking, slipping my punches. And always that left kept flicking. In time it would soften a man up.

The bell ended the round. I was a little winded but couldn't see that Doolittle was. His grin was merry.

Round two went much like round one, except that in frustration I was punching harder but again without hitting. The damn little dancing master kept flitting in and away and in again, darting out that light left, his head never where it was an instant before. He was as elusive as a loose Ping-Pong ball. I had begun to sweat.

When the round ended, the kid was licking his lips. He said, "Man, oh, man."

I came out, totally exasperated, at the beginning of round three. I would get him yet. He hit me with a left and a right and slipped under or away from my counters. Yet I knew I was getting closer. Where I had been hitting air, my left grazed his shoulder, my right the top of his head. He couldn't dodge me forever. The round ended with his fist in my face.

I had the grace to say, "You're too good for me, Ike."

"Wrong decision," he answered. "In another round or two you would have nailed me. I can't do the polka forever. Three rounds is my limit."

He went on as we walked to the shower, "I never told you, but I boxed professionally once. In the early rounds I could outbox most of them. Light stuff, you know. I never had much of a punch. One night I went against a sure-enough brawler, and in the sixth round he landed his Sunday punch. For a week I had no more brains than a cabbage. When I came to I said enough. A man's got better use for his head than to offer it up for a pudding."

We were slipping into our clothes when he continued, "Don't give up on yourself, Jase. You're damn good."

I wondered how far that reference went.

After we were dressed and had said thanks to the boy, Doolittle asked, "Feel better now, don't you?"

The fact was I did.

13

In June daylight comes early in Montana. By four
A.M. the dark has lifted, and by five o'clock the sun is
ready for its sweep.

Rousing with the first flush of day, I lay still,
hoping to go back to sleep. I put a hand to my eye and
cheek, feeling a soreness there from Doolittle's left
jabs. Slowly I began to think maybe I was feeling
better, about both my work and myself. Doolittle's
therapy may have been good medicine. Opposites came
into conjunction, it almost seemed. Pugilism and peace
of mind. Sweat and serenity. There was even an affinity
between bowel and brain. Regularity begat rationality. I
gave up on this line of conjecture and told myself to go
back to sleep.

But the murder, the two murders, wouldn't go
away. We hadn't a clue and no one to suspect. Mefford?
No sure connection. Fenner? I had crossed him off.
Antonelli? Highly unlikely. Either one of the Days? Not
from what we'd gathered. Might as well suspect Alfred
Parsons, the principal, or any one of the high school
boys. It could be one of them. Then it struck me that
we hadn't given thought to newcomers in town. What
with seismographers and drill crews at Overthrust, the
town hadn't accommodations for all, with the result that
a good many workers commuted from Midbury. And
they were a brash bunch. I would inquire.

At eight o'clock I walked to the office. The day
might turn hot later, but now the weather was a caress.

Charleston was at his desk, rereading reports. "There must be something here," he said, "but I can't find it."

"Same here."

"Don't think I'm giving up, Jase."

"Don't think I am."

He glanced up and smiled, as if he had found something fresh in my words or expression. "That's the spirit."

The reviving spirit came close to collapse when Gewald came in without asking or knocking. Clarence Gewald, state criminal investigator, or properly, had there been any grammarians in the attorney general's office, state crime investigator. We had had our fill of this character a couple of times before. He was a mule-headed bumbler whose job must have owed itself to political pull. He offered his hand to Charleston, ignoring me, and said out of his tight and righteous mouth, "I understand you need some help here."

Charleston answered, "I wasn't aware of it."

"Couple of murders, rape-killings, on your hands, haven't you?"

"We can attend to them."

"Cases unsolved?"

"So far."

"So," Gewald said as if the point were clinched. "May I see your records?"

Charleston got up, sighing, and said, "I suppose." He went to the files and got out my reports.

Gewald took them, saying, "I'll take these to my room to study. Jackson Hotel."

Charleston told him, "You're responsible."

"That's my name."

Gewald went out.

Charleston barely had time to say, "Pisswillie," before Amussen came in through the back door. "I've got my man," he announced.

"Good for you."

"I spilled him in the back cell. He's too drunk to question."

Charleston nodded, as if stalling, not making the immediate connection any more than I did.

"It's the Bar Star break-in I'm talking about," Amussen said, offended at the lack of response. "I collared the guilty party and also collected a few bottles of stolen booze."

"Where did you find him?"

"Northwest, in an old cabin by the big swamp. There was a sleepy old mule, too, but I left it."

"Good thinking," Charleston answered with a smile. "We could hardly charge it with transporting stolen goods."

I asked, "What put you onto him?"

Amussen drew himself up. "I got my sources."

I could guess what those sources were. Amussen, half kid himself, was popular with the high school boys, who, with no classes to attend, were here, there, and everywhere.

"How drunk is he?" Charleston wanted to know.

"Not just falling-down drunk. So drunk that lying down he has to hold on, if he's got enough sense to do that."

Turning to me, Charleston said, "Better get hold of Doc Yak. The man could die on us."

Doc happened to be in his office. He said he'd be right over.

When he arrived with his bag, Amussen took him back to the cell. On their return Doc said, "He won't kick the bucket, not right away anyhow. I gave him paraldehyde to ease him over the horrors."

Amussen stayed in the room, listening.

"Any chance he could be our rapist?"

"Naw. I don't think so. His liver's bad."

"On surface examination?"

"Don't be so damn stupid, Charleston. The man has liver hands."

"Liver hands?"

"Red palms and fingers. That indicates cirrhosis, and a victim of cirrhosis is dead as a eunuch."

"Sit down, Doc, and answer a question."

Doc sat. "What else have I been doing?"

"Another one, then. Would a man realize in the act that he was violating a virgin?"

Doc settled back, his head drawn in, and I knew we wouldn't get an immediate answer. He could be short-spoken or he could pontificate. He was voting for the latter. "The hymen," he told us, "is by way of being a vestigial growth. One theory is that it developed before our ancestors came out of the surf, the purpose being to keep sand from penetrating the vaginal canal. You can shoot that theory full of holes, but it remains a theory."

"Thanks."

"Now the hymen varies from female to female. More often than not, I would say, it is quite frail. Girls break it through exercise, through bike or horseback riding or skating or other vigorous pursuits. But it can be so tough that a bit of surgery is required before a marriage can be consummated."

Charleston interrupted to say, "None of that answers my question."

"Would a rapist realize he was deflowering a virgin?" Doc stuck his head out and snapped, "Jesus Christ, Charleston, I'm a man of medicine, not a psychic. You expect me to answer for a rapist? Nuts. Rapists are crazy with the heat, an apt expression by the way, and may be unconscious of everything except their own satisfaction."

"Both the victims bled?"

"And both were bruised."

"But the bleeding?"

"Any woman would bleed, virgin or not, if attacked brutally. The Stuart girl bled a lot more than Smitson, as you would expect. Penetrating her might not have been easy. That's an informed guess, but it doesn't mean anything beyond that. I say you're barking up the wrong tree, Sherlock."

"I'm not barking. Just sniffing around for a scent."

"Go ahead. Sniff your nose off." Doc managed a smile. "Good luck, all the same."

After Doc had gone, Charleston turned to Amussen, who had been standing still as a post while he listened. "Back to you, Halvor. Good work you did. Go tell Bob Studebaker, taking the bottles you found."

Amussen grinned. "Might be a bottle of good booze as a reward."

"Forget it. We'll buy our own drinks."

Cole interrupted us from the board. I couldn't hear all that he said. "Get Doolittle," Charleston told him and turned to us. "A shooting at the Fairdale corner bar. Doolittle will handle it. Jase, a break-in at the Stillwater house up the Rose River. His brother, Henry, just reported. Get on it."

"Gewald?"

"Let him simmer."

I knew the Stillwater place. A two-story house at the mouth of the canyon, it was the most ambitious dwelling along the Rocky Mountain front. Charles Stillwater, a wealthy easterner, had built it after a visit to Montana, planning to stay in it most of the year. But a couple of Montana winters had convinced him that prime weather in Montana was assured only in July and August. He closed it up for the remaining months, leaving his retired brother to keep an eye on it.

I drove along what once had been called a rocky-assed road. Since then it had been paved, and the going was better, though I didn't hurry. Break-ins, unlike murders, could wait. A couple of deer, grazing in an open field, looked up unafraid as I passed, and a porcupine lumbered into the borrow pit. I might see a black bear, even a grizzly, for June was a likely time. The day hadn't turned hot. It was just right with a soft breeze blowing.

The Stillwater house stood out from almost a mile away. With no flower planters around, no green stuff, and with the shades drawn, it seemed gaunt and closed-eyed and unwelcoming. I opened the gate, drove the car through, and tried the front door. It was locked. I went around to the back door. The latch there had been broken, and the door tightened shut with matchbook covers. Inside I met my high school self.

Feathers lay and fluttered in every room. Awkward drawings in soap—stick men with erections and what was meant to be a nude female likeness—adorned the mirrors.

And I was back in another time, when a friend and I had broken into an empty house for warmth and, warmed up, had taken to fighting with pillows, chasing and banging each other, upstairs and down, until the coverings split and feathers danced in the air. And we had drawn our own pictures, expressing our awakened and uninformed interest in sex. It all had been thoughtless and in a way innocent. It was as if we never expected the place to be visited again by anybody, and so we had fun.

On the floor I found one of those beaked, light caps that some workmen, and some boys, like to wear. It bore the initials J. W. I knew the cap. It belonged to Johnny Wilson, pal of Pat Lenihan. Johnny was the son of Will Wilson, mechanic at the Ford garage. I took the cap with me.

Driving back to town, I wished that I could simply call the boys aside and talk to them. But that would not have satisfied Henry Stillwater, and, since the boys were minors, I had to approach their fathers, a chore I didn't welcome.

I reported to Charleston, wrote a quick report and, with Charleston's approval, called Judge Joe Bolser, who was only a j.p. but liked to be elevated. He set a tentative date for ten o'clock the next morning, saying unless he heard further from me he would regard the time as fixed. Then, citing the cap as my bit of evidence, I notified the fathers. They wanted to know more than I told them. Just a boyish prank, I said, but still a break-in. I said I thought the boys would confess, though they might have to be pressed a bit. To that last Ted Lenihan, a lawyer who was father to Pat, replied, "My son will tell the truth when I ask him."

I was hanging up the receiver when Gewald entered,

again without announcement. He was carrying the folder he had borrowed. "Few questions," he said as if he had a lot of them.

He didn't get to ask them because Doolittle came in with a man in tow. "Be with you in a few minutes," Charleston said to Gewald.

Gewald tossed the reports on the desk, grunting. "See you at eight o'clock in the morning, sharp."

"Make it seven-thirty," Charleston answered evenly. "I don't like to waste the forenoon."

Gewald gave him the "Humph" again and went out.

To the man with Doolittle Charleston said, "Well, Gus, what have you been up to?" He indicated I was to take notes. Speaking to me, he said for the record, "This is Mr. August Alstedt, resident rancher of the county."

The man smiled uncertainly. "Well, Chick, all I can say is I lost my head."

Charleston's eyes questioned Doolittle, who answered, "He shot a man named Pendergast. 'Fessed up to it."

"Serious injury?"

"Nope. Flesh wound in the arm. The wife of the barman is a practical nurse. She bound it up."

"Let's hear from you, Gus."

"Happy to tell you. Can I sit down?"

"Sure. Excuse me."

Alstedt, a rather small man, was dressed in jeans and a denim shirt, and he wore cowpuncher boots and a wide-brimmed hat. These trappings remained from the old cowboy days. Even the lowliest sodbuster, in preparation for town, put them on though his closest acquaintance with a horse was a tractor.

Alstedt fingered the hat and went on to explain, "It was this way. It was the end of the day, and I had been working in the fields and thought I'd drop in to the Fairdale Bar for a bracer before going home. Pendergast was in there. He tries to bully everybody and mostly gets away with it. He started picking on me and finally

gave me a hard push that knocked me over a chair. I got
a quick temper, in particular when I got a drink in me,
and I shot him. I can't say I'm awful sorry."

"You didn't mean to kill him?"

"Hell, no. I'm a good shot."

"What makes it look worse is the fact that you were
packing a revolver."

"I can explain that. Good many rattlers in my part
of the county. The heat is bringing the snakes out. I
carry a gun to shoot them with."

"Gus," Charleston said, stretching in his chair,
"you know you'll have to face trial. I think you can
probably beat the charge, but that's no matter right
now. I'm going to recommend to the county attorney
that you be released on your own recognizance. I'll call
him now." He lifted the phone, got an outside line and
made his recommendation. "You'll have to see him
before you take off. Doolittle will go with you."

"Much obliged, Chick."

With them gone, I remembered to tell Charleston
of my vague suspicions of the oil-field workers.

He answered, "Can't hurt. Just might work out."

Charleston was stuck with that seven-thirty A.M.
date and so, for that matter, was I. Gewald, as expected,
was waiting at the door. Inside, he asked almost before we
were seated, "How hard did you lean on these characters?"

"Hard enough."

"No special persuasion?"

Gewald was dressed all in black except for a white
shirt—black suit, black tie, black shoes—an outfit, I
thought, that suited an avenging angel. His black hat
rested on his knee. In the hollow of his left shoulder
was a bulge, no doubt a shoulder holster.

"We don't beat up suspects, not in my county,"
Charleston answered.

"Humph. Now this man Mefford. I would have
given him the business."

"He's out under bond. The trial probably will be

postponed until next term of court. His lawyer has asked for a continuance."

"Not my point. How about Fenner? Did you follow up on him?"

Gewald's tone and manner were accusatory. He might have been a prosecution attorney on cross-examination. A bar of sunlight shone through the window on Charleston's hands. The fingers were interlaced, the knuckles white. "You've read the report," he said. "Beard was satisfied."

"I don't know that I am. We come to this so-called Madame Simone, the nookie bookie." His voice condemned her. "She seems like a slick article. She's holding back. That's my hunch. I want to talk to her."

"No one's standing in your way."

"I should hope not. Now I'm going to poke around. In your reports I see some loose ends."

"I'm sure you'll be able to tie them up."

The irony was lost on Gewald. He didn't know that Charleston was seething.

Gewald picked his hat from his knee, rose, and said, "See you later."

As the door closed Charleston rasped out a breath, then shook his head. "We have to put up with that knucklehead," he said. "A shame, but we don't want a hassle with the state. Lucky for him. Otherwise, who knows? I might shoot him."

I fooled away the time until the hour for the boys' hearing before Judge Bolser, then went downstairs to the courtroom.

The boys were there, in Bolser's small hearing room, their fathers with them. Also present were Henry Stillwater and Silas Wade, county attorney, who had run for attorney general and been defeated in the primary.

Judge Bolser came in, hitching his pants up on his paunch. He always assumed a severe manner at hearings, or usually did, but I knew that amusement lay behind the manner.

"Court's in session," he announced once he had

got comfortably arranged in his seat. At the side of his
bench stood a witness chair and before it accommodations for attorneys. A few of the curious had dropped in
and taken seats. Wade took charge. His first witness
was Stillwater, who described what I had seen for
myself. Then it was my turn. The boys hadn't looked at
Stillwater, and they didn't look at me. Their eyes were
on the floor.

"Do you substantiate what Mr. Stillwater has testified?" Wade asked me.

"Yes, sir. He was accurate. He might have added
that little damage was done, aside from inconvenience."

"You saw the soap drawings on the mirrors?"

"I did."

"They were pornographic?"

"I suppose you could call them that."

"Showing men and women in the act?"

"No, sir. Just singly."

The boys still looked at the floor. My gaze went to
the adults, and my thoughts to appearances and hypoc-
risy. Here they were, these grown men, males of flesh
and blood and impulse and sometimes no doubt of
forbidden indulgence—here they were, stiff as sculp-
tured saints, as if no thoughts of theirs went below the
belt.

Wade was asking, "The lock on the door was
broken?"

"It was a flimsy latch."

I had done what I could for the boys. I saw myself
in them, shamed and guilt-stricken as I had been in
that year gone by.

Wade called on Johnny Wilson to testify. Johnny
answered in monosyllables, speaking down his front,
saying just yes or no. When Wade asked him if they had
broken in, Johnny hesitated and replied he didn't think
so. He couldn't remember.

When Pat Lenihan was called and asked the same
question, he answered, "We may have. I guess so." I
knew he was trying to be truthful while covering for his
partner.

At the conclusion Judge Bolser gave the boys a stiff lecture, mostly about the offense of breaking and entering. He tended to shy away from the pictures, maybe not wanting to act the utter hypocrite.

We filed out, no one speaking. The fathers looked stiff and chagrined. The boys went off in different directions, away from the adults and away from each other.

So it had been with me. Disgrace. The end of everything. Lasting shame. And then Charleston had put a hand on my shoulder.

I hurried after Pat. My hand went to his shoulder, and Charleston's words came back to me. "I understand, Pat. It's almighty hard, being a kid."

The boy shot one glance at me, saying nothing, and walked on. But I thought his shoulders were a little straighter.

14

The drunk who had broken into the Bar Star was led in the next morning. Just before his arrival I had asked Charleston, "Wonder where Gewald is?" He had answered, "Not hard to guess. He's snooping on the trail we left, quizzing everybody."

The drunk, brought in by Doolittle, could walk but that was about all. He looked at us with inflamed eyes while his face twitched. He licked his lips with a tongue like a chow dog's. His hands and arms shook as if attached to a jackhammer. He took a chair uncertainly. He might have posed as the ultimate example of excess in alcohol.

Charleston gave him the choice of a lawyer or of standing mute, with the warning that whatever he said could be used against him. The man kept nodding, though I doubted that the words got through to him. He did say his name was Tom Burke. Home? Just around, here and there. Charleston told him he was charged with breaking and entering as well as theft. "What do you have to say about that?"

Burke licked his lips again. "Thirsty is all."

"Thirsty now or thirsty then?"

Burke looked up with a sudden despairing hopefulness. "You got a drink, friend?"

"Hold on. You don't deny the charges? You did break in and steal the whiskey?"

"Anything you say." His shaking was making me twitchy. "Jesus, have a heart."

Charleston reached into his desk, got out a bottle

and glass and poured three fingers. "This is just for a bracer," he said. "The doctor will be in later with more medicine."

Burke's trembling hand was reaching out. Doolittle put in, "Better use both hands, partner. It's not the floor that wants a drink."

Burke took the glass in both hands, but, even so, the glass clinked against his teeth and some whiskey ran down his chin.

"Take him back," Charleston said, talking to Doolittle.

On his return Doolittle said, "A case of wet brain or close to it."

The phrase was new to me. Doolittle added, "Booze, too much of it, kills the brain cells."

"District court sits here tomorrow," Charleston said. "I'll try to get his trial advanced."

"He'll get maybe six years and be out sooner than that," Doolittle said. "Out and free to follow his chosen career."

I filled in at the board for a while, read through my reports, went out on one trifling call, and had dinner with Mother.

The night's business at the Bar Star had barely begun at seven o'clock, but three young fellows already had seated themselves in a booth and were drinking beer. From their dress and the wild shags of hair on two of the faces I gathered they were oil-field workers. The third man was smooth-shaven and appeared maybe a little older than the others. I bought a beer and took a booth next to theirs.

As I walked to it, they looked at me casually. Without my uniform or badge I would pass as a mere civilian.

I didn't have to wait for the talk to veer to the subject I was interested in. They were already on it—which wasn't too strange since it was the common concern in town. "Eight to five they'll never catch him," one of the men was saying.

"It's too damn bad that he wasted her," another said.

"Yeah, a pretty little piece like that. You've seen her?"

"Just once or twice, flittin' around after school or sometime. What about you, Mr. Bill?"

I peeked over the back of the booth and saw that Mr. Bill was the smooth-shaven one. He said, "I knew her to speak to her."

"Lucky you. I bet that put a tent in your pants."

"She was jail bait, wasn't she?" one of his companions asked.

"Sixteen, the paper said, but what the hell? She was big enough and ripe enough. A neat piece of ass."

"I wish you guys would shut up, you, Les, and you too, Frank." I knew from the voice that it was Mr. Bill speaking. "Here a nice young girl has been murdered, but you don't give a damn about that. You're just wishing you had got to her first."

"Now, Mr. Bill, you shy away from the subject like that, and we'll be thinkin' you done it." There was a teasing deference in the voice.

"Just say I'm tired of crotch talk."

"Which don't leave much to go on about."

At this point I got up, took my half-finished beer and slid in beside Mr. Bill. The three looked at me with surprise if not hostility. One of the whiskered men had better soil for a crop than the other. The hair on his face bushed out and fell well down his chest.

"I couldn't help overhearing you," I told them. "I'm a deputy sheriff, and I'm on the case."

"Some company we're keeping," the smaller beard said.

"Pipe down, Les," Mr. Bill said. He turned to me. "How's the case going?"

"I wish I could say we're making progress. We're not."

"I'll collect on my eight-to-five bet," the man called Frank said. Mr. Bill waved that remark away. I went on, "Maybe something has come to your attention. Maybe you have a reason, however slight, to suspect someone. Maybe you've seen or heard something."

"And you expect us to squeal?" Frank asked.

"If I had anything, I'd tell you," Mr. Bill said. "So would these two guys. They like to play lunkheads, that's all."

"I don't like bein' suspected, and I don't want any of our guys to be suspected." Frank's tone was dogged.

I asked, "Did I say I suspected you?"

"No," Mr. Bill answered, "but you do, and you're right. You have to suspect everybody until you nail down the right man." He was speaking more to his pals than to me. "Right, Mr. Deputy?"

"Yep. I'll see you. Keep an eye out, will you?"

I went home and got into bed and, with one thing and another, fiddled away most of the next day. At four o'clock I was on my way to Overthrust. A hare-brained trip, I thought, but good to be taking. Bluebonnets decorated the slopes and balsam root the hills, and in a gulch I breathed the fragrance of chokecherry bushes in bloom.

My first call was at the friendly sheriff's office. He was seated at ease behind his desk, chewing on a fat cigar. He had a long upper lip like a horse's and, with the cigar in his teeth, might have been eating cottonseed cake. There was the look of decay about him, like that of a one-time athlete who had graduated to rich food and whiskey. He wore a revolver, cased to a shiny cartridge belt.

"Good afternoon," I said. "Remember me? Deputy Sheriff Jason Beard."

He regarded me lazily. "A man wouldn't know it from the looks of you. No badge. No uniform."

I took my badge from my shirt pocket and showed it to him. "Want me to run home and get my uniform?"

"You got a loose lip."

"Sorry. Let's not start on the wrong foot."

He made a vague gesture toward a chair, not offering to shake hands, still slouching in his seat.

"You know we have a couple of unsolved murders."

"Too bad."

"It's all of that."

He munched on his cigar, his eyes showing only a mild interest if that. He managed to say, "Yeah."

"Some of the workers from Overthrust bed down in Midbury."

"It's legal, ain't it? Or are you too good for the like of us?"

I pushed on. "Some of them know or have seen Virginia Stuart. She's the second victim."

"I been known to read."

"So I thought maybe you could help us. Are there any pointers here? Any bad actors you've had trouble with? Anything at all that might help me?"

He straightened then and put his cigar in a tray. He pointed a finger at me. "I keep an orderly town. You can bet your ass on that. I got things under control. Anyone gets out of line gets pulled in. Got that?"

I nodded. He went on, "In this office we draw a sensible line, making allowance for young squirts and high spirits. Some allowance, that is."

"That makes sense, but what you've said doesn't help me."

"Didn't aim to. You won't get help from my office because it ain't there. You think we would close our eyes to a goddamn murder?"

I thought he might but didn't say so.

"You got the run of the town far as I'm concerned. Look it over. See for yourself. After supper the boys usually have a beer or two at The Gusher. You have anyone or anything in mind, go there and nose around, though I don't know as I'd want to. Some of our young fellers are pretty quick on the trigger."

"Not guns?"

"Not by a damn sight. It's tempers I mean."

He was baiting me, and I rose to the bait. I said, "The Gusher it will be. Thanks." He retrieved his cigar and slouched back, chewing.

To kill time, I called on Madame Simone. At this hour the house was quiet. Dressed in a gray outfit, she looked trim and ready for business. She invited me to have a drink with her, and I did. I told her about finding Mefford and the charges against him, and his making bond and being free for the time being at least.

"I hope he doesn't come around here," she said. "Brutes like that are bad for business."

"And maybe for girls, or one of your girls, though we haven't been able to tie him to that case."

"Keep trying."

"You haven't any new ideas. No clue since I saw you?"

"Not a smidgeon."

I found a fair-to-good restaurant and ordered a steak and baked potato. Except in top-flight eating places the menus in Montana always specify "potato and vegetable," as if the ubiquitous spud had been disowned by the vegetable family. I had a choice of corn or peas, both from cans, of course, and voted for peas. The food wasn't bad, and I took my time over it.

At seven-thirty I entered The Gusher. It was a rundown place with a lively business. A placard on the mirror stated, "All our bartenders are half-fast." A juke box was playing at full volume, and voices shouted over it. A pool table stood at one side of the room. Two men were playing, the click of the balls lost in the hubbub. The place smelled of spilled beer, smoke and bodies. Eight young men were lined up at the bar, drinking beer mostly. Dressed in checked shirts and jeans and field boots, they were hairy as English sheep dogs, as if whiskers were the necessary proof of manhood. Among the crowd I recognized Les, Frank and Mr. Bill, who presumably didn't need the proof.

I edged into the line at the bar and ordered a beer from a barman with fat hands, who slid bottle and glass my way, saying, "A clean glass for a new customer."

Eyes began turning to me. The players at the pool table racked up their cues. The juke box ceased its hyena howling. There came a watching silence. Then a young fellow with immense shoulders and a head that ran out into his neck said to me, "New around here, ain't you?"

"Not from far away."

"What you doin' here?"

"Drinking a beer."

"Why not drink it at home?"

"Simple, I'm not home."

"You want some advice, drink up and fuck off."

Frank, the haired wonder, interrupted, "Hey, he's from Midbury, and he's a deputy sheriff."

"I already knew that from the smell. Now you, pig, take your slop outside."

"I like it here."

Frank spoke again, "He thinks one of us done in that Midbury girl."

The big man asked me, "That so?"

"Not particularly. Right now I suspect everybody."

"But especially us. That's why you're here. Boys," he announced, "make way. I'm throwing the bastard out."

I slipped off the stool. The onlookers had drawn back, forming a rough circle. Maybe they didn't intend to gang me. The big man followed my thoughts. "Just you and me. No help needed, not by me."

I asked, "How you want it? Fists, rough and tumble? What?"

"Any goddamn way you please. I'm tellin' you, though. Once you're down, I'll kick the shit out of you."

He came toward me, grinning, his heavy arms hanging low, crooked a little at the elbows. I had time to think he had won the right to brag that he could whip any man in town.

I had to beat him fast, if I could. The longer the fight, the more likely that onlookers would want a piece of the action.

He moved into me, still smiling. I spun half around and kicked back and up, karate fashion. My shod foot caught him square in the face. I spun back. He had staggered and gone to his knees, his nose flowing blood.

"Son of a bitch," he said, shaking himself upright. "Try that again, and I'll tear your leg off."

I kept him back with a left jab, then hooked my right to his belly just below the rib cage. The wind went out of him with the sound of a blown tire. He bent over, sucking for breath, then rolled to his back, his breathing shallow and fast.

Frank and a couple of others started forward from the circle. Mr. Bill hurried ahead of them. He took Frank by the arm. "No ganging! Be sports. Duke got what he asked for."

At this moment the sheriff entered. He looked at the tortured body, then at the men, then at me. "What's going on here? Jesus Christ, you crippled a man."

"He'll get his wind back."

"I ought to run you in."

"But you won't. And next time, if you want to play tricks, make double sure your bully boy."

They were silent as I went to the door and let myself out. I got in the car and started home.

There was no joy in humbling a man, even a brawler, and no dividend in my trip.

All in the day's work.

15

As if we weren't busy enough, what with court in session and two deputies waiting to testify, Gewald showed up at midafternoon the next day. Entering the inner office, he was all business. "That Madame Simone will be here at five o'clock," he announced.

Charleston looked up from his desk. "What for?"

Gewald took off his hat and gave what for him was a smile. "To identify Mefford. That's one of the loose ends."

Charleston's head moved from side to side, slowly, as if in rueful acceptance of stupidity. He asked, "She's coming willingly?"

"She'll be here. I told her I'd close her down if she wasn't."

"You had the authority?"

Gewald sat down and pointed a finger. "I've learned to bluff. Any law officer should. Use your position, man. I didn't have authority. I assumed it, and it worked."

"So."

Gewald rose, putting his hat back on. "I've got to get Mefford here. I'm going after him right now."

"Take Jase with you."

"I don't need a boy to look after me," Gewald said after casting a glance at me. "I can take care of myself."

"Doubtless, but Jase goes with you or follows right after you."

Gewald gave a mock salute and answered, "Yes, sir, Mr. Sheriff. I'll look after him."

I knew why Charleston insisted I go along. He was afraid that Gewald, once in control, would try to beat a confession from Mefford.

We took an office car. I drove, and Gewald sat in the passenger seat. I thought a few good jounces might lower his arrogance and so took the short cut.

We had an inspiring conversation. I said, "Nice day," and he answered with his phlegmy grunt.

But it was a nice day. Wild flags waved in the fields and harebells decorated the roadside. The sun, not yet at its July glare, was asking things to grow. As the car climbed, the picket-pin gophers of lower down gave way to Columbian ground squirrels. The latter were more wary than the picket-pins and less likely to get run over.

I eased to a stop at some distance from the trailer. "We may surprise him," I told Gewald, who grunted again. From behind the trailer I heard the knock of an axe against wood. We eased around to the back and caught Mefford chopping kindling. Gewald asked under his breath, "That's Mefford?"

At my nod he called out, "Mefford! We want you. We're the law."

Mefford stepped toward us, the axe swinging from one hand.

"Drop it! Drop that axe."

Mefford didn't.

Almost before I realized, Gewald whipped out his pistol and fired. The bullet struck the axe head and went singing off. The axe trembled from Mefford's hand.

"That's a sample. Come along," Gewald said.

I wondered whether the shot was just lucky and decided it wasn't. Chalk one up for Gewald. He could shoot.

To the right of us Mefford's woman came climbing up from the gullied stream, a willow pole in one hand and a couple of trout on a forked stick in the other. Her eyes asked questions.

Gewald called, "Stay right where you are." He

moved the automatic pistol by a fraction. "No trouble from you. Hear? Come along, Mefford."

As Mefford came closer, I stepped between the two. No pistol whipping if I could help it.

"We're taking you in," Gewald told Mefford. There was a slow burn in Mefford's eyes, like live coals under ash. He didn't ask why, but Gewald informed him, "Little matter of identification."

He had a moment for me. "Now, Beard, your good sheriff ought to hold him, but will he?"

"Not without evidence."

"I know. Me, I would hold him for a couple of days and soften him up. But that's not the point now. Your kindly sheriff might think this man should be brought back to his camper."

"Could be."

"I'll save you a trip. Mefford, climb on to that bike I see there and go ahead of us. Not more than fifty yards, or I'll shoot you off it. At that range and more I can pick the eye out of a magpie."

I imagined he could.

Returning to town, we took the longer and smoother road, with Mefford looking back to make sure of his distance and Gewald in the seat by me, the pistol shining in his hand.

We trooped into the inner office. Charleston was alone at his desk. He looked up without speaking. The clock on the wall said five P.M.

"No Simone?" Gewald asked.

"No Simone. Have seats, you all. Hello, Mefford."

Mefford gave a bare nod of his hairy head. "What's this time?"

"Ask Mr. Gewald."

Gewald said, "You'll see. That woman is supposed to be here. I'll go get her if I have to."

We waited, quiet, Gewald fuming, for ten minutes when the board announced a visitor.

Madame Simone entered with a sort of aloof dignity, nodding to me. She was dressed like a business woman, like the chairman of the board of the Y.W.C.A. might be.

"You're late," Gewald said.

"My car gave out at the edge of town. I had to walk."

She regarded him as she might regard a dog turd on her clean carpet. Then her eye fell on Mefford, and she said, "You wanted identification. That's him."

"Not so fast. Hold up for some questions. This is for the record." He glanced at me as if he expected me to get busy with paper and pencil. I didn't.

"You say your name is Simone."

"I told you once that's my name."

I brought up a chair for her.

"Assumed or for real?"

"It's my name."

"You operate a disorderly, an immoral house?"

"Not disorderly."

"No? A fight occurred there."

"Fights have occurred in the United States Senate, but I have never heard it called a disorderly chamber."

"Quit quibbling. At least you admit your business is immoral?"

"Some would say yes; many would say no."

"I vote aye. Let's see. The fight took place on the night of June four. Tell us about it."

"That man there—" She pointed.

Gewald interrupted her. "You identify him? You're positive? He caused the fight?"

"I'm sure. Who could mistake that hair? Who could mistake that figure and face? Besides, he has some of the same clothes on that he wore then."

Mefford's eyes fixed themselves on her. If looks could kill, she would be dead.

"And on that same night, the night of June four," Gewald resumed, "one of your girls was raped and choked to death?"

"That night or early the next morning."

"That was the girl, as I understand it, that he had wanted to take upstairs?"

"Yes."

"Didn't you put two and two together?"

"I tried to, but I wasn't sure I had two and two."

Charleston spoke then. "Even if her answer had been four, it couldn't be enough for us. The question leads nowhere."

"I'm doing the questioning," Gewald said.

"So you are. So you are."

I added "supercilious" to the adjectives that described Gewald.

Madame Simone broke in. "I identify this man. Isn't that enough?"

The slow fire in Mefford's eyes blazed. He motioned toward Madame Simone with a clenched hand. "It was you, damn you, who put the fuzz on me. You caused the trouble." He turned his face to Gewald. "Where's the proof? Where's the goddamn evidence? You and the sheriff here take the word of this pussy peddler. A little old fight in a whorehouse, and she points the finger at me. That's all you have."

"Shut up, Mefford," Gewald told him. "A couple of days together, just you and me, and I bet I'd have more."

Mefford turned his glare back on Madame Simone. I thought there was a wild and hunted hatred in it.

"You going to hold Mefford?" Gewald asked Charleston. Apparently he was through with his questioning.

"No known reason to."

"Too bad. All right, Mefford, get on your bike and go."

After Mefford had gone, the rest of us got up. Gewald left us without speaking, no doubt to fry other fish we had fried already.

Charleston said, "Thank you for coming, Madame Simone. There was no need for the cross-examination. I won't apologize for this office, since it was none of our doing, but I do apologize for the profession, if law enforcement is a profession."

"Don't blame yourselves. I don't know which of those two men I dislike most."

"Flip a coin. It might stand on edge. You must have rubbed Gewald the wrong way. He had no call to get after you as he did."

"He rubbed me the wrong way when he called at the house, and I suppose I was short with him."

"So he had to get back at you. That's Gewald."

We fell silent until I said to Charleston, "With her car broken down, Madame Simone has no way to get home. I thought I would take her."

Charleston nodded and kept nodding as I ushered her out.

16

On the ride to Overthrust I seconded what I had decided already. Mefford was a stupid and vengeful brute who acted on impulse. There was, I figured, thinking of his glare, more than a fair chance that he would visit Madame Simone tonight. So I would spend the dark hours patrolling the premises.

We rode along companionably, the madam and I, talking of this and that, avoiding references to Gewald and Mefford, though they were in my mind and doubtless hers. Out of a silence she asked, "You have a girl, Jason?" It was the first time she had called me by my first name.

"I suppose you could say so."

"Treat her well then. Never regard her as a matter of course."

"That sounds as if you might be bitter. About men."

"Not bitter. Just realistic. Men are men."

She let the statement ride before she continued, "I'm realistic about wives, too."

"Tell me."

"Wives tend to become a dreary lot."

"All of them? Why?"

"Not all of them, but I'll tell you why. What with household work, laundry, meals, pregnancies and child care, they let themselves go, or a lot of them do."

"Go where?" I asked to lead her on.

"To nowhere. They get to be mere drudges. They grow careless of personal appearances. They eat too

much and get fat. Some of them take to the bottle and
grow into household drunks. Or they make careers, if
they have time, of bridge and club memberships. Anything to get away from the house and the old man. But
I'm talking too much."

"Not for me."

"I was about to add, they grow waspish."

"And it's all their fault?"

"Quit prompting me, Jason. All right. Let's not
talk of faults but facts. The fact is that a great many
marriages are destructive, both to husband and wife.
The men expect too much. They are thoughtless. They
can be demanding. They want a reasonably tidy house.
They want meals on time. They expect clean clothes.
All that and more."

"Is that unreasonable?"

"Not to a man."

"You paint a sad picture."

She spread her hands for emphasis. "It's the way of
things, Jason. The stupid way of things, and both
partners are caught in the current."

She looked out on the landscape. The view was fair
under the lowering sun. A couple of clouds lazed in the
sky.

She sighed and resumed, "I suppose you could say
that's where I come in. Through the girls I give the
men what they want and haven't had. Call it sex, but
it's more than that. It is tenderness and willing compli-
ance. With his ardor renewed and satisfied, a man feels
better about himself, about his life. I bet I've bolstered
more marriages than I've broken."

"How's that?"

She gave me a quick smile, then turned her head
away. "I've talked more than enough. You don't want to
hear more."

"I'm the judge of that. What's this about bolstering
marriages?"

"Here goes then. Remember you asked for it. With
his sexual needs met, with the knowledge that there's
something of the old Adam still in him, a husband

grows more tolerant at home, more thoughtful, more helpful, less critical. The old girl isn't so bad after all. He may think of his honeymoon days and act accordingly."

She was trying to justify herself and doing a good job of it. I wasn't in a mood to pick holes. I said, "Hard on your girls, though."

The remark set her off again. With spirit she answered, "Not a bit of it. None of my girls ever was or will become a common prostitute. Too much class. I have never recruited a girl. They come to me. I weed them out. I won't take a sloppy girl or a dull one or an alcoholic or a virgin, if there are any of those left. My girls intend to marry, God help them. They'll be better wives because of experience. They won't blunder into marriage. They'll choose with their eyes open."

We were nearing her house now, and it was time to change the subject. "This man Mefford—" I began.

"Do we have to talk about him?"

"For a minute anyhow. If you see a man skulking around your place later, don't be alarmed. It will be me."

"You? What in the world for?"

"Just on the chance."

"What chance?"

"That Mefford will try to visit you."

"Surely not. And, Jason, you don't need to do that."

"Sheriff's orders."

"That's not so. I heard what he said."

"That's what he meant," I answered, thinking of Charleston's repeated nodding as we left the office.

"You and he. Two peas in a pod. Thoughts open to each other. Mind readers."

"Sure."

"I can't order you away. But look here. It's dinner time, and you haven't had anything to eat."

"No more have you."

"I have a cook, and we're here at my house. Would it sully you to break bread with me?"

"A square meal never sullied anybody."

We entered the pink parlor, and Madame Simone went to a door and called out, "Irma, we have a guest for dinner." The answer came back, "There's enough and more."

Returning, Madame Simone said, "Now, Jason, don't feel hurried. I have a rather full schedule tonight, but business usually doesn't begin until after dark. About ten o'clock on these long days. If you need to freshen up, go through that door. There's a bathroom on the right."

When I came back, she had drinks poured, remembering that I preferred bourbon and water. I sat in a pink chair and she on the pink sofa. After sipping, she asked, "You really think it possible that Mefford will try to come here?"

"I wouldn't be surprised. He has it in for you. He's impulsive. He acts without thinking."

"He must be mad."

"He blames all his troubles on you."

"I've run into that reaction before. It's common enough. If you've made trouble for yourself, blame it on someone else."

"A sort of scapegoatism. Yep."

We had finished our drinks when the cook came in. She was a short woman of middle age and a complexion that suggested Indian blood. She said, "Dinner is ready."

"Thank you, Irma. This is our guest, Deputy Sheriff Jason Beard."

The woman's mouth opened to a quick breath. "The law."

"The friendly law."

We followed Irma through a rather large dining room in which sat an oblong table. The table had a neat cloth on it and some glassware. Overhead was a chandelier.

"I hope you won't mind eating in the kitchen," Madame Simone said. "Sometimes guests bring snacks or a bottle or two, and I shoo them in here."

"Fine. Food tastes best in a kitchen."

The kitchen was big and well-equipped. I counted a refrigerator, a freezer, a dishwasher, an electric stove, and other appliances before I sat down. The table was ample, covered with what I took to be linen though it probably wasn't.

Irma served us beef stew, rolls, and a slice of melon each. "Nothing very elaborate," Madame Simone said, "but I hope that it holds you."

My mother might have envied the rolls, and the stew was excellent, seasoned by a cook who knew flavors. As I took a second helping, I said, "That's a mighty fine stew, Irma. Sure hits the spot." She looked away from me, tucked her chin against a shoulder and smiled.

We took our time over the food, talking idly between bites. When we were through, Madame Simone asked, "Coffee? Brandy?"

"Nix on the brandy, thanks. It might make me drowsy. Coffee will be fine."

Irma had stood demurely while we ate and talked. At last she asked timidly, "All right I go soon as I wash up?"

"Of course, Irma. I'll drive you home."

I said, "I'll take her."

"No indeed, Jason."

"The sheriff doesn't like just anyone to drive office cars."

She put her hand to her mouth and laughed. "You win. I forgot my car's in the garage."

So I drove Irma to her home. It was a tiny, neat house on the edge of town. She thanked me and said, "See you in the morning if so you're there."

On my return I told Madame Simone, "I'm going to scout around while there's some daylight left. Forget about me, but be careful about whom you admit. Keep the doors locked. Make sure of your caller."

"He wouldn't dare come right in."

"He did before. Where's your bouncer?"

"He came while you were gone. He has a room in

the basement where he can smoke and drink beer. If I need him, I press a button that rings him."

"Better tell him about me."

Outside I began prowling. The sun had gone down, but banners of red, salmon and yellow decorated the western sky. June was a time of long twilights.

Madame Simone's house was big. In addition to the basement and first floor, it had a second floor large enough, I calculated, for six bedrooms, more if they were small. In the back, shielded by a half-circle of cottonwoods and dwarf pine, was a discreet parking lot. There was a smaller one at the front. The place had a front, back, and side door.

For my watchout I chose a place at the side of the house, some distance uphill from it. From here I could see all three doors and note the cars that arrived. And I could rest my back against the trunk of an old tree that would help conceal me.

There was nothing to do then but wait.

I sat down, vaguely wishing that I smoked. Smokers spent a lot of time with cigarettes and pipes. I chewed a grass stem.

Slowly the banners in the west faded. A star dared to come out. And I waited.

It was a night for starshine. Almost all at once it seemed, there they were—the Big Dipper, the North Star, the glimmer of the Pleiades, the sparkle of a million others.

Lines ran in my head. "One by one, in the infinite meadows of heaven/Blossomed the lovely stars, the forget-me-nots of the angels."

Longfellow was a rhythm smith but a pretty sappy poet. There was Emerson who said that if the stars came out only once in a hundred years men would bow down before the wonders of heaven. No bowing down for me: I was on stakeout.

The front light came on, a dim pink against the shadows of earth. A car slid up to the side door, and a girl came from it, said something and went in. Almost at the same time another car purred to the parking lot.

Its driver walked around to the front door and after a minute was admitted. The night's festivities had begun.

And so it was going—a girl now and a girl then, a car now and a car then. And so it would go until the last spent man departed.

I didn't know the girls and couldn't identify the men. They appeared to be middle-aged or about that, which would fit what I had gathered. They could afford the price. Kids couldn't.

A shadow moved from in front of the house. A live shadow, it stepped through the shadows of grass and bush, moving with purpose. It grew to be a man, name unknown. He marched toward me. I didn't stir but made ready to spring. The man halted. "Get up! State your business!" I recognized the voice of the law, and I recognized him. He had a revolver in his hand.

"Yes, sir," I said, scrambling up. "You know me. Deputy sheriff from Midbury."

"Answer the question. What you doing here?"

"Voluntary guard duty. I thought Madame Simone might be in danger."

"What in hell made you think that?"

"It's a long story, but a man we have under bond made threats against her. You can ask Madame Simone about me."

He put the revolver away. "I make a tour around here nearly every night."

"How did you spot me?"

"Owl eyes," he said, "and the shape under the tree wasn't like what I knew it was. Then I got a glint, I think from your wrist watch. Starshine on it."

"Damn good work."

He scratched his jaw. "Say, ain't your name Beard?"

"Jason Beard."

"And ain't you the guy beat up our town bully?"

"I had a fight at The Gusher. Wasn't much to it."

"Maybe not, but a couple of other guys have belted him since you showed the way." He gave a satisfied laugh. "Tickles hell out of me. On account of the sheriff liked him and used him on some rough stuff, he thought he was better than us poor deputies. But no longer, by God. You dimmed his light."

"Then I'm glad."

"Say, Beard, forget I spoke tough to you. And how about shaking my fist?"

We shook hands, and he moved down toward the house whistling.

The night crawled on. A girl left, and a man. A star fell, a blazing streak and then nothing. I moved to ease my aching butt.

From the rear of the house a figure appeared. It walked to the side door and stood still. I got up and stepped toward it, moving as quietly as I could. To its back I said, "What's your business here?"

The figure spun around. I saw then that it was a young man with a beard that hadn't grown up. He couldn't have been more than twenty years old. He said, "What business is it of yours?"

"My question comes first."

"All right. I'm waiting for my girl."

"You look young to be a pimp."

I saw the punch coming, a right-handed, round-house swing. I caught his wrist, pulled him to me, jerked him half around and got him in a half nelson. That hold isn't hard to break if you know how. He didn't.

I forced his arm up between his shoulders until he squeaked. "Calm down now," I told him. "I'm a guard." Then I let him go.

"You called me a pimp," he said in a voice of grievance.

"What are you?"

"I'm engaged to be married, that's what. My girl works here."

"You let her?"

"Are you a sure-enough guard?" He rubbed his arm. "You're tough, anyhow."

I showed him my badge. In the starshine he could at least see it was a star.

"All right then," he said. "We got to have a stake,

my girl and I, before we get hitched. I'm an apprentice
carpenter, which don't pay much. To help along, my girl
comes here when she's asked. She's a typist."

"When do you intend to be married?"

"Pretty soon now."

"Will she work here afterward?"

He drew himself up. "Are you crazy? Of course
not. Marriage is what they call a sacrament. It will be
just her and me."

The girl came out then. She gave him a quick
embrace and said, "We can go now, Johnny," in a clear,
young voice.

I moved away and sat by the tree again. What with
this boy, Gewald, Madame Simone, and assorted others, I was being given a broad education in the sexual
moralities.

After the last girl and car had left, I heard Madame
Simone's voice calling me in. "Shift's over," she said as I
entered. "High time for you to have a drink."

I thought so, too, and took it and sat in the pink
chair. "Hardly an eventful night," she said, raising her
glass. "It seems your time's been wasted." Her green
eyes smiled at me.

I answered, to be original, "Better safe than sorry."

"I never did think Mefford would have the nerve."

By and by I took a second drink.

She said, "When you're through with that, you'd
better be going along. It's late, and I suppose you have
to work tomorrow."

She had hardly finished when the sounds came—
two plunky hits, as of bullets, and the slight tinkle of
falling glass. Then I heard the shots.

I ran out the door. I heard a motorcycle start and
then its throty roar as it receded. It left the night
silent.

I went back in, meeting Madame Simone at the
threshold. "I was afraid for you," she said.

"Upstairs," I said. "Let's see."

"It sounded like my room. I leave the lights on."

We hustled up the stairway. From what I took time

to see of the room, it looked comfortable and neat. In a window at the side were two starred holes. Slivers of glass ground under my feet.

"It would have killed someone, namely you. But it's over. Come away."

We stepped back down the stairs and stood in the parlor. "No danger now," I told her. "Mefford has had his revenge. He's satisfied."

"You mean you can go?"

"Yes. It's safe."

She moved to me and took one hand in both of hers. Looking into my eyes, she said, "You're a fine man, Jason." Her voice faltered. "It will be a lucky girl who gets you." Suddenly her face softened, and I thought I saw an infinite sadness there.

I kissed her on the cheek and went out to my car. I never happened to see Madame Simone again.

17

The days and nights that followed strained our manpower, demanded overtime from all of us on the force, and left us groggy for sleep. With circuit court in session, Amussen and Doolittle had to be available as witnesses, the one against the drunken whiskey thief and the other against the rancher who had shot a man. God knew when the cases would be called. The judge was a dawdler, an amiable and ineffective man who operated on the theory that justice demanded time and coaxing. The pace of proceedings meant that witnesses spent hours waiting to take the stand. More than that, the county commissioners were in two-day session with Charleston often in attendance.

He took time to listen to my oral report of the night at Madame Simone's. At its conclusion he said, "Good enough, Jase, but don't write it up yet. Keep it to yourself. If Gewald hears about those shots, he'll be hell-bent to bring Mefford in again. I don't want that now. No purpose to it yet. And no proof Mefford was on that motorcycle and fired the shots."

Busy as we were, Charleston tried to keep a couple of men on night patrol, a chore he didn't assign me presumably because I was on special duty. The night patrol rode around for reassurance, since the town and county were edgy, parents keeping sharp watch on their girls. Who could say that the murderer wouldn't strike again? Charleston doubted the probability, not the possibility, of a third crime. On the streets men were saying, not quite in criticism, that at last he faced problems that were too much for him.

Under the circumstances it was largely Cole and I, assisted by Blanche Burton, who held down the office. Off and on Gewald would come in. He would brush by the watch command, enter the office as if it were his by right of position, pace around, scan the record, perhaps take a note or two and go out, barely speaking.

Yet I managed one night to spend a couple of hours with Anita. She had called to invite me to dinner, and I resolved to go even if I went to sleep at the table. Over chicken and dumplings and rhubarb pie we talked about the rape-murders, about the weather, about her livestock, with Omar telling us about pastures, the likely size of the hay crop and the general health of his charges.

He left us soon afterward. I helped with the dishes and said thanks, I had to be going. At the door I kissed Anita's responsive mouth, but when I pressed against her, she pushed me back, saying, "I told you once, when I do it I do it for keeps."

Driving back for a turn at the office, I thought of the good job awaiting me. I thought of my age. I thought of Anita. Keeps didn't seem a bad proposition.

I was at the office, yawning, by ten o'clock the next morning. Cole was yawning at the board. I heard Charleston's greeting to Cole before he came through the door. The damn man had a habit of looking fresh and fit. He went to his chair and rubbed his hands as if with satisfaction. "You won't believe it, Jase, but at last we have some leeway in our budget."

"Good. But we manage to get along as it is."

"Barely at the best of times. At the worst, as of now, we're in bad shape. You know it. Stop yawning."

"Yes, sir."

"I'm going to put Blanche Burton on the force full time. What do you think about that?" His eyes questioned me, waiting for an objection, or perhaps for approval.

"Fine with me. She knows the routine. I guess she could handle herself against rough stuff."

"I'm betting on it. But now, Jase, no male chauvinist protest?"

"Not from me. I can't speak for the others."

"A lightened workload is a great convincer." He took out a thin cigar, lighted it, and presently pointed it at me. "That's not all. I'm putting three women on as watch commanders, three of them, to be relieved on their days off by Blanche. She can train them to begin with. It's a shame, wasting manpower on that board. A trained woman can function there as well as any man."

"No question. . . ."

"So be it, then. I want you to visit Blanche, tell her about her appointment, and ask her for suggestions about the women prospects. I'll be strongly inclined to accept her recommendations."

"Go now?"

"When better?"

I rose, but he halted me with, "Visit the prospects maybe. Might be best."

I drove to Blanche's small house. It stood on a fifty-foot lot freshly mowed, with planters of petunias and pansies in bloom.

She opened the door to my knock and asked me in. The place was neat, not too feminine, as if she had no time or taste for frills. She motioned me to a black Boston rocker and took a seat on a sofa.

"Official call, Jase, or just social?"

"Make it both. First of all, the sheriff wants to put you permanently on the force. Full time, I mean."

"Why," she said with a movement of her hands that was not a flutter, "that's wonderful. I accept."

"That's one thing."

"Conditions?"

"Nope. Just more work for you. Mr. Charleston wants to add three women on as watch commanders."

"That's sensible, but where do I come in?"

"You're the nominator, subject to approval. Know any likely prospects?"

"I certainly do."

"You'll have to train them, so be careful."

"I can think of half a dozen offhand."

"Names?"

"How many middle-aged widows would you guess we have around here? How do they spend their time? With bridge games, that's what, and with sewing circles and with morning coffees and the trading of recipes they'll never use and maybe a volunteer stint at the hospital. Anything to fill up the time." Her eyes asked me for understanding. "They're desperate, Jase. Some of them are. Their lives are so empty."

"Gossipy old ladies wouldn't do."

"You ought to know me better than that."

"Your suggestions then, Blanche."

"I've been thinking ever since you opened the subject. Here are two I recommend. One is Jane Innis, the other Margaret Stafford. Know them?"

"They're pretty solid citizens, as I remember."

"You can repeat that. The other one might not strike you that way. She's an unmarried mother."

"With a child to take care of."

"No. The grandparents have taken over the baby and are delighted with it."

"And she's delighted to shed the responsibility."

"Not so. And don't be impossible. The grandparents are not people of means, not by a long shot. So the girl does housework to support herself and help support them and the child. She's a bright girl."

"Not too bright, getting caught pregnant."

"She was deceived by a man she won't name. Now remember, Jase, one fall doesn't make a whore out of a girl. Have you ever heard of redemption?"

"Not lately."

"She was valedictorian of her class. She's intelligent, industrious, and, despite your doubts, decent."

"I suppose I ought to see her."

"Not the other two?"

"I'm sure they'll pass."

"Let me see if I can find her."

She excused herself and went out of the room to phone. When she returned, she said, "She's house-cleaning for Mrs. Gray today, and it will be all right if we call."

At Mrs. Gray's home a sprightly old lady answered the bell. She said, "Hello, Blanche. Come in. You want to talk to Susan Strand, you said. I'll call her."

"Thanks, Mrs. Gray, and do you know Deputy Sheriff Jason Beard?"

"I know his mother, of course, and his father when he was alive. But am I in some trouble?"

I said, "Not a bit of it."

She left the room and presently a girl entered. She had on working clothes and a smudge on her nose. Her straight hair was tied back.

"Susan," Blanche told her, "let me introduce Deputy Sheriff Jason Beard."

The girl looked me straight in the eye and held out her hand. "I hope the law isn't after me." In spite of the words she looked unafraid. She had a small, stubborn nose and, I thought, suffering eyes.

"Yes," I said, "the law is after you, thinking you might fit a job that is open."

She had us sit down but kept standing herself. "A job?" she asked.

"This is exploratory," I said. "The questions are: Do you want the job and do we want you?"

"What job?"

Blanche cut in. "It's really just operating the switchboard and working the radio at the sheriff's office. Answering questions and requests for help and radioing the reports to the deputies."

"I know nothing about switchboards, and all I know about radio is to turn the set on."

"That's where I come in," Blanche said. "I'll teach you."

The girl looked down at her soiled clothes. She raised her soiled hands and regarded them. She murmured, "A job."

Differently gotten up, I thought, she could be pretty. She was pretty already. But prettiness wasn't a credential. The stubborn nose, and honest eyes, the open manner—they could be.

Blanche put in softly, "Mr. Beard knows about your trouble."

"Everybody does." She turned her face full to me. "There's no funny business in this job, is there?"

Again Blanche broke in, "For goodness sake! Funny business? In Mr. Charleston's office? Of course not."

"I had to know. I can't rely on trust."

Blanche's eyes questioned me, and I gave her the go-ahead. "We're satisfied," she told the girl, "and we hope you will be. I'll notify you when to report, and Mr. Charleston will explain about salary."

Susan looked me full in the eyes again, though her own were shiny. In a low voice she said, "Thank you."

She turned before I could say to her, "Thank Blanche Burton."

Gewald was entering the inner office when I came in. I followed him. Charleston was looking out a window, his face thoughtful, but walked to his desk and sat down when we appeared. Without invitation Gewald took a seat. "I've talked to Mefford's brother," he announced.

"The one who put up bond?"

"Yep. First name's Giles. Business man and doing well. Real estate and insurance."

"What was the purpose?"

Gewald gestured with a bony finger. "Background. Background. He told me a lot."

As if we were eager to hear, he went on, "He's younger than our Mefford, a sort of baby brother. That's why he put up bond. I mean when they were kids Mefford protected him from the bullies. Broke one boy's jaw, but that was juvenile stuff and nothing came of it."

Charleston said, "Uh-huh."

"Now Giles told me his brother was always self-willed and hot-headed and, though he didn't like to admit it, not too smart. Mefford's been charged a couple of times, assault and battery and such, but spent just one week in jail. That's our weak-headed law for you."

"Interesting," Charleston said, not meaning it.

"What's more interesting is this." Gewald used that finger again. "Long as I was in the big town, I thought I'd question Antonelli, that music teacher. But he wasn't home in his apartment, and no one, not even his son, knew where he was. That mean anything to you?"

Charleston gave a flat "No."

"It might. It might. Anyhow I've told you."

Gewald hitched himself up and went out the door.

Charleston leaned back and folded his hands over his stomach. "You know, Jase, that man's thorough. Give him that much credit. All he needs is a new personality."

"And to quit thinking everyone's guilty."

"Now what about those women for the board?"

I told him about the prospects, and he answered, "Good. Sounds good. So does the idea of dinner. Knock off, Jase."

18

The next day was what I called indignation day. It was as if the men arrived by arrangement among themselves, though developments showed otherwise.

First on the scene was Gerald Fenner, the Overthrust attorney, who had given the sapphire to Laura Jane Smitson. He came in, grim-faced, and stated to Charleston, "My name is Gerald Fenner. I'm a lawyer." His nod to me was abrupt.

Charleston said, "Yes," and offered his hand, which Fenner affected not to see. "Please sit down, Mr. Fenner."

"Briefly, for what I have to say won't take long." He was looking Charleston square in the eye. "A citizen's complaint, Mr. Charleston, against the breaking of confidences and the harassment of innocent men."

"Those are serious charges."

"Not so long ago I gave your Mr. Beard here some highly confidential information, not to be used unless vital to a murder case. Now I find it is public knowledge."

"What leads you to that conclusion?"

"A man named Gewald, representing you, I take it."

"You take it wrong. Gewald does not represent this office."

"Then who? Then what?"

"The state. He is the criminal investigator. As an officer of the law he will or should keep that information confidential."

"But he came by it through you. You can't deny that."

"I don't. Of necessity our records are open to him."

"You could keep them out of his hands."

"On the contrary. The law is the law, as you must know. You may ask why I don't boot him out. Few things would give me more pleasure. But I'm impotent. I can't fight the state, not to any advantage. Power and politics enter there."

"And you have to think of your political future."

Charleston's face went tight. His mouth was a straight line. He leaned forward, and the tone of his voice was enough to draw up the stomach. "That remark is uncalled for. A gratuitous sneer. Good day, Mr. Fenner."

Mr. Fenner moved uncertainly, taken aback by the force of the words. "I only meant—" Then, out of character, "Oh, shit, Mr. Charleston, forget it, please. The objection is sustained. You have my apologies."

"I don't apologize. Mr. Gewald's activities are none of my doing."

"He has the manners of a Hitler *gauleiter*. His questions are not so much questions as accusations."

"I'm aware of that. Anyone he interviews has my sympathy."

Mr. Fenner was recovering his composure. He let himself smile. "I'd welcome the opportunity to cross-examine him sometime." He rose. "All right, Mr. Charleston. My apologies again to you and to Mr. Beard. No confidence betrayed."

He let himself out.

I followed him part way. Blanche Burton, at the board, was wasting no time drilling her crew. Susan Strand sat at her side. Blanche had arranged her program in two-hour hitches at different times of the day, morning, afternoon, and night, thus giving her recruits variety. This was Susan's second hitch.

Blanche was saying into the phone, "Now don't worry, Mrs. Wilcox. We have patrols out. They'll pick up anyone out of line."

She hung up and said to Susan, "Old Mrs. Wilcox reports a loiterer in her block. She's always afraid someone has broken into her house or is about to break in."

I asked, "Afraid or hopeful?"

Blanche smiled. "A bit of both, I'd say."

I was turning away when Alfred Parsons, the school principal, hustled in. "Mr. Charleston here?" he asked abruptly.

I nodded and showed him through the door. Charleston greeted him and told him to have a seat.

Parsons sat, breathing heavy. He wasn't beaming today. He was steaming. A little more, and the furnace might blow up. "It's an outrage," he said. "A downright outrage."

"What is, Mr. Parsons?"

"That man named Gewald, working out of this office."

"What about him?"

"For one thing he's agitated young Pat Lenihan into a state of extreme anxiety, virtually charging him at least with complicity in Virginia Stuart's death. The boy came to me trembling, almost in tears."

"Why not his father?"

"Mr. Lenihan is a strict and stern man, and the boy's been in trouble once, you know, with breaking into that house. He was afraid to consult his father, so came to me. I have a good rapport with my boys." The last was said with a self-satisfaction that nudged into his anger.

"Is that all?"

"Isn't it enough? But no, by the infernal, it isn't all. Gewald questioned me. It was his blunt implication that I knew more about the girl and her death than I had revealed. It was with difficulty I restrained myself. As an educator I can't afford violence. So, Mr. Charleston, what are you going to do?"

"Nothing."

"Nothing? That's incredible."

With patience then Charleston explained as he had explained to Mr. Fenner.

At the end Parsons said, "To use the vernacular, that's a pretty kettle of fish."

"Isn't it? But we're not the cooks."

"I can hope he's through with us."

"I believe I can reassure you on that point. I doubt he'll come back."

Parsons had the courtesy to give us thanks before he went out.

Charleston and I had lunch at the Jackson Hotel and came back to the office. Once seated, he said to me, "You didn't take notes?"

"No. Sorry if you meant me to."

"Your memory's good, though."

"Good enough, I guess."

"Then write up this morning's proceedings. They'll make one report I want Mr. Gewald to see."

I got busy. Charleston went out, came back, went out and came in again. It was along toward the tail end of the afternoon when we received our next complaint. It was voiced by Mr. Duncan Stuart.

He came in, erect as always, as if iron pride stiffened his spine. The day was warm, but he wore tweeds. He stood before Charleston like a post, but I could see his trousers twitch to the trembling of his legs. I knew his control had slipped even before he said, "Domnation to all of you! Domnation to your office and to your men!"

"Before we go to hell, Mr. Stuart, won't you sit down. How about a glass of water?"

"Forget that."

"Do take a chair."

Mr. Stuart perched on the edge of one. "Knowing what I know—"

"And we don't. So tell us."

"Gewald, he said his name was. I call him a bastard. Aye. An utter bastard."

"What's he done now? By the way, have you spoken to others who have complaints?"

"To whom would I speak? No. You're evading the subject."

"You were going to tell us?"

"He came into my house, that high and mighty man." Mr. Stuart swallowed the beginning tremble in his voice. "He insinuated my Virginia was not what we thought. He implied she was loose, that low life! If I had been able I would have thrashed him. Aye, I would have beat him senseless."

"It's as well that you didn't."

"You would say that, Charleston. You are to blame. I hold you responsible."

Charleston made his explanation then. It was becoming almost rote.

At the end Mr. Stuart said, "But that is incredible. It stands against reason."

"It's the truth."

"I will think on it and decide for myself." He went to the door, still stiff, and went out without thanks.

The end was not yet. Hardly had he left than Old Doc Yak came in, grinning ferociously. He plopped himself into a chair. "Let me congratulate you on your crew, Chick," he began. "Your man Gewald, now—"

"Hold it right there, you old quack. He's not my man, and you know it."

"Your man, Gewald," Doc went on without heed, "he came to see me. We had a nice, friendly visit."

"I can imagine."

"Oh, yes. He questioned my professional competence. How could I be so sure Virginia Stuart was a virgin? Had I sought a concurring opinion? At the end I told him nature had made a mistake, putting his anus where his mouth should be and vice versa. I threatened to kick his teeth in. It took him a moment to transpose his parts as I had suggested, and then he knew I meant to kick his ass out."

Charleston said, "Brave words, Doc. Brave."

"Not so brave." Doc gave that ferocious grin again. "I happened to have a scalpel in my hand at the time. So he departed."

19

Gewald stood, reading my reports. They included an account of the protests without a word softened.

There were just the three of us in Charleston's office. The time was early afternoon the next day.

Gewald laid the file aside after reading the last page. "A good investigator is bound to ruffle some feathers," he said.

Charleston replied drily, "So it would seem."

"You were pretty rough on me, my friend, but I understand. You have to think of your constituency."

I expected Charleston to explode. Instead, he said, "Every vote counts."

"So be it. I have something else on my mind. You haven't told me about the bone-pickers."

Charleston looked puzzled.

"Over west somewhere. Near what I believe is called Clay Hill."

"You mean the dig, the dinosaur dig?"

"Yeah. You didn't tell me."

"Why the interest?"

"They're foreigners, aren't they?"

"Just from out of state. They were here last year."

"I'm surprised you haven't questioned them. You can't just take them for granted. They're possibilities."

"No stone unturned, huh?" Charleston was rearranging things on his desk. A man other than Gewald would have known his patience was being tried.

"That's the idea. I'm going to make a run out there. Beard here can show me the way."

I said, "I take my orders from Mr. Charleston."

"Oh, for Christ's sake! Charleston?"

"All right," Charleston answered with heavy forbearance. "Better get it over with, Jase."

"I'll take the state car with Beard as guide."

Gewald drove with concentration. Had there been a pea-sized pebble on the pavement, he would have seen and dodged it. When we came to a dirt turnoff, he grasped the wheel with both hands.

On this late-June day the sun burned down with the glare of July. Opened, the car windows let in blasts of hot air.

The camp, such as it was, came into view—a rather large tent, a tepee, a couple of sleeping bags turned out to air, a car and a pickup, a case of empty beer cans, a tarpaulin held down by rocks over presumable supplies, two shovels, a pick and a wire screen.

Down the slope from it, beyond an outcrop, two men and three girls were working. Near them was a pile of mineralized bones.

Gewald got out of the car, walked partway toward them and called out, "Whoever's the boss, would you come and talk to us?"

"Why, sure," one of the men said. "What about?"

I climbed from the car.

"Just a few questions."

They had all looked up. One of the men left the group and came toward us. He was a muscular man of fair complexion, and I noticed that, unlike the other man, who wore only shorts, he had on a shirt and a pair of pants. "Yes, sir," he said. I judged him to be only a little older than I. His nose was peeling from sunburn.

"We're officers of the law, hunting for a murderer," Gewald told him. "Combing every bush, we are."

The man smiled. "We're grave robbers, not murderers. But all right. There's a little shade at the side of the tent. Then fire away."

Between us and the shade a white shirt hung from a tent rope. Its tails were rusty, the color of old blood. Gewald snatched it up. "What's this?"

"I had a nosebleed. Touch of the sun maybe."

We had halted short of the shade. "A nosebleed," Gewald said. "Can the others verify that?"

"Only in part. What are you getting at? I was working away from the rest, a hundred yards or so. I told them about it afterward."

"How much later?"

"Next day, I guess. A man doesn't make a to-do about a nosebleed. I had only my shirt to wipe my nose on."

Gewald moved into the shade. He must have been burning up with that black suit on. "Interesting," he said. "Why all the clothes? Your partner's in trunks."

"Because I can't seem to tan. I just burn."

The man sat down. He didn't seem perturbed. Gewald pressed on. "When was the nosebleed?"

"A week or more ago."

"Say ten days?"

"That's close enough. The shirt didn't seem worth washing even if I could get the bloodstains out."

"It was ten days ago that one Virginia Stuart was raped and strangled."

The man's face opened and closed to his words. "For God's sake, you don't think it was me!"

"Where were you at the time of the crime?"

"How do I know? The days run together in this work." I could have added that the days run together in any work. "What day of the week was it?"

Gewald turned to me for the answer, and I said, "A week ago last Wednesday."

"Then I was right here. We work six days a week, taking Monday off for shopping."

"And sleep the nights through, I suppose. By the way, what's your name?"

"Yule, Richard Yule."

"You heard about the girl's murder, it's evident."

"Naturally."

"Did you know her?"

"Slightly. I bought her a Coke once. Winsome is the word that described her."

"Too winsome, it seems."

Yule got up. "Is that all?"

"I'm afraid not." Apparently Gewald was thinking all of a sudden of the protests or remembering that I was on hand, for the answer was civil enough.

Gewald went on, still in that reasonable way, "Since you're innocent, I hope you won't mind going to town for a blood test."

"To see if the shirt and I match. Is that it?"

"If you don't mind?"

"What good would it do me if I said no? But, sure, I'll go to town with you."

"You ready then?"

"Let me tell the crew." He walked down the slope, spoke to the others, came back and climbed into the car.

Gewald drove without speaking over the sun-stricken bench and down into the valley to Midbury. After that one outburst, Yule didn't appear worried. He whistled for a bit, then lit a cigarette and, puffing, said to me in the back seat, "This is an insane business," to which I answered, "The heat alone is enough to drive a man crazy."

Jane Innis was alone at the board, proof enough of Blanche Burton's training. "Mr. Charleston just came in," she said.

Charleston was just sitting down at his desk. He looked up, taking us in.

"I want some blood tests," Gewald said, seating himself. "This young man says he had a nosebleed about ten days ago. He says he wiped it off with his shirt tail."

Charleston held up a hand, palm out. "Not so fast." His eyes went to Yule. "Be seated, please. You have given your name?"

"Yes. Richard Yule."

"You're a paleontologist?"

"Yes, again. Degree from Harvard. We're working here on a grant."

Gewald asked, "What's a paleontologist?"

Charleston answered for Yule. "A student of fossils." He spoke again to Yule. "I hear you've made some exciting finds?"

"Far beyond what we expected originally. We've come upon what might be called a dinosaur village, a regular colony. Nests, eggs, young dinosaurs, adults."

"Out of my league," Gewald put in, shaking his head.

"Most people find it fascinating, once they know," Yule answered him. "It's part of the history of the planet we walk on. It's part of the evolutionary chain. I suppose you could say dinosaurs were one of nature's mistakes since they all died off. But they were here once in numbers we can't estimate."

"When was that?" Gewald asked.

"Seventy million and more years ago."

Gewald said as if it were a joke, "Before my time." He added, "I'm interested in the here and now. I want the blood tests, yours, Yule, and the shirt's."

"If they match," Charleston told him, "it won't prove much. Many people have the same type of blood."

"But if they don't match?"

"They'll match."

"We'll see about that. Call the county health nurse, Beard. We'll need a sample."

I waited for Charleston's nod before I called. The nurse wasn't in, but an assistant was. She came from upstairs, an older woman named Mrs. Dawson who, I knew, had found the routine of hospital work too much for her years. She was still expert, though, and had blood in a vial almost at once.

On her departure Gewald said, "I'm taking this and the shirt to the hospital. Then I'll call on that stiff-necked Scotchman and find the type his daughter had."

I knew from his glance what Charleston wanted so I said, "I'll save you the trouble. Just a minute."

I walked to the outer office and called Mr. Stuart. "This is Jason Beard, Mr. Stuart," I said. "I'm sorry to disturb you, but there's a chance, a very slim chance, that we're on to something. Can you tell me your daughter's blood type?"

"No. I cannot. It was an emergency delivery. It came on my wife all at once. There was no time to get her to a hospital, and I couldn't rouse a doctor. I called the wife of a neighbor, who was something of a midwife, and together we delivered the baby. Everything went well."

"And Virginia never had her blood typed?"

"She never did to my knowledge. She was always healthy. Not a day in the hospital."

I started to thank him, but he interrupted, "What is this, Mr. Beard? What do you have?"

"I'm afraid nothing. Just a bloody shirt in all likelihood from a nosebleed."

Back with the group I reported what I had learned.

Gewald got to his feet. "We'll want the tests regardless. Yule, please stay here." He went out with the vial and the shirt.

"A nosebleed?" Charleston said to Yule.

"That's what it was."

"They can be bad."

"I'm learning that. A nosebleed, and here I am a suspect. What kind of man is that Gewald?"

"Gewald is Gewald, and no helping that, I'm afraid. But let it go for now. I'm interested in your discoveries. Tell me more, please."

"If I can forget the fix I'm in."

"I would dismiss it."

"I'll try to. I said we were finding fossil bones on bones. All of them so far, or nearly all of them, are the remains of Duck Bill dinosaurs, rightly called Hadrasaurs. They were plant-eaters. The nests and the presence of immature creatures along with adults suggests family care, which you don't find among reptiles. In addition their very size argues against their being cold-blooded. After a chill how long would it take tons of cold-blooded meat to limber up? So we reach a conclusion, tentative but persuasive, that dinosaurs were warm-blooded animals."

"That's pretty convincing."

"And at odds with prevailing theory. I said we were finding only Duck Bills. That's not entirely true. We have unearthed just one hollow bone, a small piece, like the bone of a bird, and we are asking ourselves if it might be Pteranodon."

"You have me there."

"It was a flying beast covered, we rather think, with white hair or fur."

"I see. Anything else?"

"I wouldn't be altogether surprised if we came on the bones of Tyrannosaurus Rex, the most terrible creature nature ever produced."

"And they all died. What from?"

"It's just conjecture. Some might say climate, and do, but a change of climate would not account for the concentration of bones we're finding. They surely would be scattered. We are flirting with the idea of a great mud slide."

The discussion ended with the return of Gewald. "You're type O," he said to Yule on entering.

"I could have told you that."

"No make on the shirt. No necessary equipment. I've made arrangements to send it to the state lab."

"And I'm getting hungry," Charleston said. "Jason, do you feel like driving Mr. Yule back to camp?"

"No need to," Yule answered. "One of the gang is coming in for supplies." He grinned. "We ran out of beer."

Gewald rose and left the room.

"So I'm free, am I?" Yule asked.

"I never yet held a man on a charge of nosebleed."

20

I had come to the office early, only to find from Susan Strand that Doolittle, Amussen, and now Charleston had been summoned to circuit court as witnesses. Apparently the judge had finally reached our cases. Cole, Susan said, was out on a call, not an important one. I stuck around in case I was needed.

It wasn't until after lunch that I was. Then the connecting door swung open. Cole stood there, trying to block it, but the Mefford woman squeezed by him, screeching, "Where's the big man?"

She stumbled in, her face bruised and bloody, one shoulder hunched. A cracked leather purse swung from her free hand. Her clothes might have come from the town dump.

"I caught her coming in," Cole said.

"The big man," the woman scratched out. "I got news for him."

"You need a doctor."

"Hell with that. Get the man."

"Won't I do?"

"No, by God! He makes the deals."

"Take a chair, then."

I telephoned the judge's chambers upstairs. Luckily someone answered. I said I had to speak to the sheriff, and the voice answered, "I'll see." When Charleston came on, I told him, "The Mefford woman's here, all beaten up. She won't talk to anyone but you."

"Be there," he answered and in about a minute

entered the office. After one glance he said, "You need attention, Mrs. Mefford."

"Don't Mrs. Mefford me. I'm not Mefford's woman, not anymore. I'm Gracie Jones, like I told you once."

He sat down and used the phone. "Doc Yak's not in," he said, dialing again. "Miss Blakesly, can you come to the sheriff's office at once, bringing your kit?"

Miss Blakesly was the county health nurse, with offices over ours.

The woman said through bloody lips, "He'll be after me."

"Take it easy."

She put a hand to a cheek that was swollen to half again its usual size. The eye was closing. The other cheek bore a ragged cut. Her mouth was broken at one corner. She didn't move that one arm and shoulder. She touched the shoulder with the other hand. "That's where the bastard kicked me."

"Wait for the nurse."

In less than a minute Miss Blakesly, a plump young woman, all business, entered with her nurse's case. After a glance she said, "My goodness, were we caught in a baling machine?" From her case she took cotton, alcohol, gauze and tape. "Hold still now. This will sting a little."

"I'm past feelin'," the woman said.

Charleston sat silent at his desk.

The nurse went on, "Your mouth really ought to have a stitch or two in it. This will have to do until then." Gently she moved the woman's arm and felt of the shoulder. "I can't find any break. But here, I'll fix a sling until the doctor sees you." The sling in place and the forearm resting in it, she packed up her things, smiled and went out to our thanks.

The woman's face, patched, bruised, colored white, red, and beginning purple, put me in mind of a child's first attempt at finger painting.

"Now," Charleston said, "maybe we can talk. Your name is Gracie Jones, and you live with one Mefford?"

"Lived. Did live."

"Tell us about it. Why are you here? What do you want?"

"I want to be safe."

"Mefford beat you up?"

"You got eyes."

"How long have you lived together? How long have you put up with him?"

"Skip the questions. I got a proposition."

"Answer the questions first."

"Lived with him? This last time just three months. Off and on before then."

"But why?"

"Mister, I got nothin'. I never had nothin'. Know what? I can spell my name, but that's all. When you got nothin', most anything looks good. A body gets tired of washin' dishes in some greasy-spoon joint or swampin' out saloons where men ain't careful where they spit. Then along would come Mefford, bound for one place or another, and I just took off with him. I know. Damn fool me. But what else was there, me bein' what I am?" A tear squeezed out of her closed eye.

"How long has this been going on?"

"Ten years, maybe, but just now and then. Nothin' lastin'. In the beginning he used to lay me, as you polite folks would say, but I was younger then, just twenty-five or so and I guess not too bad to look at. Now all I do is clean up and cook and hope he keeps his temper. But by God no more of that, I swear."

"This last beating must have been the worst?"

"That's one reason I'm here. He was drinkin', and he just blew up over nothin'. With me laid out, he took his bike and vamoosed."

I put in, "Vamoosed?"

"He can't have gone far," Charleston said. "I would have heard."

"Oh," the woman told us, "he'll just be sleepin' it off in the shade someplace. Him and that camper is pals."

"How did you get here?"

"It don't matter, but I walked to the road and a man picked me up. I didn't know him. He wanted to take me to the hospital. I told him the sheriff."

"So now?" Charleston asked.

"So now lock me up safe."

"Not him?"

"I said I had a proposition. You open to a deal? Kind of tit for tat like?"

"How can I tell?"

"Look." With her free hand she fumbled to open her purse. The purse fell from her lap, but in her hand was a pin with the biggest sapphire in it that I ever saw.

Charleston breathed, "By God."

She clenched the pin in her hand, not offering it to him. He asked, "Where did you get it?"

"In his cache. It's built into his bunk, and the eye don't catch it without lookin' close. I didn't know what was in it, for he keeps it locked, but after he took off I broke it open. There was a little money there, too, drinkin' money, I bet, but I left it. When he finds it out, he'll be boilin' mad. He'll come after me. I know him."

"And all you want is safety in exchange?"

"Just lock me up as long as I say. Mad or not, he can't hurt me there."

"It's a deal. I'll have a doctor call on you later."

The woman dropped the pin in his palm.

"Jase," he went on, "take Miss Jones back and make sure that she's comfortable."

On my return he said, "We got him, Jase, got him dead to rights. Now locate Doolittle and Amussen. If they haven't testified, ask the county attorney to move to adjourn. If I know the judge, he'll be glad to oblige. He gets mighty tired, sitting on the bench."

I was on the phone when the two deputies came in, court having been declared done for the day without urging.

Charleston got us all into his inner office, Cole included. He explained and showed the pin with its big, sparkling sapphire. "Now we go get him," he said, "all of us except Cole. Ken, keep after Doc Yak. We can't neglect our witness."

"Yes, sir, or no, sir, I guess I mean."

"I want her put up at the Jackson Hotel once we've collared Mefford. He can't curse her there."

Charleston stood up. "Carry your sidearms." He went to the cabinet and took a Winchester shotgun from it.

We traveled in two cars after a final briefing. "Amussen and Doolittle, you go ahead. Circle round in back of the camper. Then sneak up if you can, one to each end of it. Jase and I will follow and tackle the place from the front. Go on. We'll give you time to get positioned."

They took off, and we after them, going slow. All Charleston said was, "Here's hoping he hasn't made tracks."

At six o'clock the sun wasn't thinking much about bedtime. Some lazy clouds floated over the mountains. Our speed was about 25 miles an hour.

Charleston slowed the car when the camper came in sight. "They'll have had time," he said. He pulled up maybe 35 yards from the front side of the camper and sat looking. "Bike's there. Good. He hasn't found out about the sapphire or he'd be gone." He stepped from the car, taking the shotgun with him. He marched ahead a piece and called out, "Mefford. Come out. Sheriff's office."

All he got was silence.

I saw no sign of Amussen or Doolittle. Their car, I thought, must be hidden on the far side of a clump of quaking asps that grew beyond the camper.

"Stay here," Charleston said, walking forward. I picked up a rock about the size of a baseball. I swept his restraining arm aside and dodged in front.

"Mefford," I yelled. "Come out or get blown up. There's a grenade in my hand. I'm counting to three."

From behind me Charleston said, "Out of the way."

"One. Two. Three. Here goes."

I threw the rock, thankful for my pitcher's arm. It made a satisfying thump on the undercarriage of the camper. I shouted, "Down. Down everyone," and hit the dirt. An instant, and then Charleston did the same.

Mefford popped from the camper. He stepped down, a shotgun in his hands. He looked at us and looked to his left. That was a mistake. Moving fast for his bulk, Amussen charged from his right. Mefford had time only to move the gun a fraction before Amussen's arms went around him. They swayed there for a moment. The gun fell without going off.

A bear hug from Amussen would make a fence post cry for mercy.

Now from the left of the camper Doolittle came racing, cuffs in his hand.

We got up, Charleston and I. He said with a trace of a smile, "You damn smart fool you." We walked ahead. Mefford wasn't saying anything. His face spoke for him. Doolittle dodged into the camper and came out with the .22 rifle. He picked up the shotgun. "Damn tidy place," he said cheerfully, "except where he messed it up."

Charleston said, "You boys made the catch. How about bringing him in?"

"Gladly. Yes, sir. It was you, though, you and Jase, that risked hide and hair."

Now Mefford said through his tangle of whiskers, "You sons of bitches."

Doolittle and Amussen took him off. In the car on the way home Charleston called the office. "Blanche," he said after identifying himself, "Cole still there?"

Her voice came back, "I knew it was you. Yes, Cole's just leaving. I was late getting here."

"Ask him to take Gracie Jones to the Jackson Hotel. Tell him to tell her we've got Mefford under arrest. She'll be safe. The county will pay the hotel bill."

It was well past supper time when we arrived at the office, but Charleston wasn't about to quit work. He herded us all into the inner office, Mefford included. I made ready with pad and pen.

Charleston sat at his desk. "Sit down, you," he said to Mefford. Doolittle and Amussen stood, looking and listening.

"Mefford, I'm charging you with murder. You're entitled to a lawyer . . ."

"Or I can keep my mouth shut . . ."

"But whatever you say can be used against you."

"I'm all buttoned up."

"Why did you resist us?"

"Jesus Christ! I'll say this much. First, that joker there"—he looked at me—"he knocked me out. Then you sapped me. And another of your men took a shot at me. What the hell? Expect me to invite you in?"

"All right. That's by the way. It's murder we'll talk about."

"Talk away."

"You killed the Smitson girl."

"I did, huh? Where's the proof?"

Charleston took a key from his pocket and unlocked a drawer of his desk. He held out his closed hand, opened it, and there was the sapphire pin. "Proof enough."

Behind his whiskers Mefford's mouth opened. He sucked in a breath. He got out, "How in hell?"

Charleston just sat, holding the pin.

Then Mefford broke out, "Oh, that thievin' bitch. She turned me in, the goddamn cow. I'll wring her fuckin' neck."

"You'll have to wait quite a while. Meantime, she'll testify against you."

"No one would listen to her."

"We'll see. Now let's talk about the other murder, the rape-killing of the Stuart girl."

"Not by a damn sight. You can't pin that one on me."

"But the first one I can."

"Goddamn her. She thought she was too good for me. Too high-toned for the likes of me but was still selling her ass. I won't take much of that stuff."

"Hardly any of it, huh?"

"She had it coming."

Charleston said, "That's enough for any jury. Amussen, take this character back and lock him up tight."

Amussen yanked Mefford by the arm and marched him out.

Charleston was opening his desk when Amussen returned. He brought out a bottle. "No one's on duty. I figure we're entitled to a celebration."

We drank out of paper cups without ice. Then Charleston went on, "I want to take you all to dinner. While you wash up and get ready, I'll make reservations. Suit everybody?"

I stepped to the outer office, got an outside line and told Mother I wouldn't be eating at home but would be in later with good news.

We walked to the Jackson Hotel. It was seven-thirty, a late hour for dinner in Midbury, and the dining room was empty. A waiter was expecting us, though, and he asked, "Ready to eat, Sheriff?"

"Four stomachs all set and ready, and bring us some good red wine."

"All here but old sour puss," Doolittle said.

A small smile settled on Charleston's face. "Mr. Gewald is busy. Has been all day. He's looking for Antonelli, but he won't find him."

I asked, "How come?"

"Mr. Antonelli is visiting friends at Flathead Lake. It seems he felt out of sorts and left home without informing anyone."

"A little bird told you," Amussen said.

"No. Mr. Antonelli himself. He called me last night to see how we were making out."

The wine came first. Charleston poured, got up, holding out his glass, and said, "Here's to a first-rate crew."

Amussen lurched up. "And to a first-rate chief." Their eyes came to me. It seemed we were playing rounds with our toasts. I said, "Second the motions but drink also to luck."

Doolittle topped us, saying, "To whatever gods there be, thanks for Gracie Jones and we."

We laughed and drank, and the waiter served us tenderloin steaks, baked potatoes, not canned but garden-fresh peas and salads that were not all lettuce. About to pitch in, Charleston paused and asked the waiter, "The lady upstairs, Gracie Jones, has she eaten?"

"Oh, her. They say she's keeping to her room."

"Take her a plate just like ours."

We were hungry and merry, full of relief that a job was done, and we laughed and talked while we ate. Only at the last, with plates cleaned and appetites satisfied, did Charleston sober our mood, saying, "Tomorrow's another day. Virginia Stuart's another case. Let's get some sleep."

21

Outside the courthouse the next morning I met the two reporters coming from the sheriff's office. They had learned of Mefford's arrest late in the night and had awakened Charleston, then me, for details. Now they were looking for follow-ups. I passed them, saying, "You know as much as I do." They had one big story and no doubt were keen for more. That was the way of reporters. One sensation wasn't enough: they wanted another and another.

Susan Strand was at the board. "Nothing important," she said to me. "Mr. Doolittle and Mr. Amussen are out on calls. It's Mr. Cole's day off."

It had been a long time since anybody had had a day off. "Mr. Charleston has a visitor," she went on. "She just went in."

I knocked and entered. Seated opposite Charleston was Miss Effie Douglas, whom everybody knew. She claimed powers of divination. She wore an outfit that history may have remembered. On her head was a flat-crowned hat with a wide brim from which a fringe hung. She waved a hand from a blousey sleeve.

"Oh, Jason," she said, "I've just started to explain to the sheriff, hoping to help him. I have told Mr. Charleston that I am something of a mystic and seer, though he knew that already."

I said, "Yes, ma'am."

"I have been to the scene of the crime and I visited the Stuarts, who, I must say, were rather cool."

Charleston sat back without speaking.

"The scene is blurred," Miss Douglas continued. "I get a flash or two, but nothing really helpful except for one thing."

She wanted us to ask what that was, and I did.

"The culprit is a local product. He lives right here in this community. That much I know."

Charleston said politely, "We'll bear that in mind, with thanks." He got to his feet, dismissing her, and she bustled out.

For a while after the events of last night the office was comparatively quiet. Tom Burke, invader of the Bar Star, had been tried and sentenced to two years in the state penitentiary. The case against August Alstedt, charged with shooting and wounding, had been dismissed for lack of prosecution witnesses.

At eleven o'clock, Gewald came in and promptly sat down. "Antonelli's flown the coop," he announced.

"Is that so?" Charleston asked idly.

"Not hide or hair of him."

"Things have happened in your absence. Mefford's in jail, charged with the murder of the Smitson girl. We have a virtual confession."

"I suspected him all along. You leaned on him."

"No." Charleston went ahead then to tell about Gracie Jones and the sapphire.

As he told the story, Gewald began to slump like a leaking tire. The old arrogance seemed to be sinking. And for a moment I could feel sorry for him. All his blundering diligence exercised for nothing. All his work, his energies, undone by a break.

That was the trouble with being broad-minded. It produced a weakening sympathy for the other side. It softened convictions.

At the end Gewald drew a deep breath and straightened his shoulders. "It solves both cases then," he said, as if brightening up. "Press Mefford hard enough, and he'll confess to the Stuart killing. I knew it was him."

He stepped toward the door. "Comes at a good time for me. Got a telephone call last night. The men in Custer County need help. So I'll say goodbye."

"Goodbye, Mr. Gewald."

Gewald walked out, leaving the connecting door open. I turned to watch him go. Charleston could see from his position. From the side of the switchboard a foot came out. Gewald stumbled over it and fell on his hands and knees facing the exit. He snarled out, "What's the idea?"

"I'm so sorry," Susan Strand said. "Sitting so long, a woman has to stretch now and then."

Gewald had climbed up. "Watch your feet."

"I said I was sorry. Now may I give you the same advice?"

Maybe that was the way of women, I thought. Maybe they were more set in their convictions and readier to act on them. Certainly Susan Strand was. She would do.

Gewald slammed the door, leaving.

Charleston settled back in his chair. "So much for that. Mr. Gewald lacks one quality."

"Just one?"

"I'm speaking of imagination, of the ability to analyze and compare."

"I might guess."

"Don't strain. The rape-killing of Laura Jane Smitson was a matter of spite, of revenge, of getting back at a woman who had snubbed him. The crime against Virginia Stuart was strictly sexual in nature. Mefford wasn't and isn't guilty of that."

"Yes, sir. How is our one and only star boarder?"

"Quiet but sullen. Appetite good."

Then, to make conversation, I said, "I met the two newshawks outside."

"Yeah. They wanted to get a picture of our star witness, but I nixed that. I said if they tried they could expect no more cooperation from this office. I won't have them pestering her, not at least until she looks like something human."

"She's kind of on my mind," I told him. "She strikes me as not so bad an old girl."

"Even though she conked you with the frying pan?" He smiled as he spoke.

"Even so."

"You're right, considering. I am thinking of dismissing the charges against her."

"Good. I thought I'd call on her this morning."

"Fine. Go ahead."

At the desk of the Jackson Hotel the manager, name of Jack Turner, held me up. "What's the score with that old bag upstairs, Jase? I took her breakfast to her just to see. She's had the hell beat out of her. That's plain. And she dresses like the tag end of a fire sale."

"Just treat her right. She's important."

He wanted me to say more, but I made for the stairs.

Gracie Jones opened the door just a crack, saw me, and swung it wide. "Welcome to my fancy quarters."

"They taking care of you?"

"Just fine. I'm livin' high."

She looked better, if not recovered. The black eye was prominent, but the abrasions were less noticeable, and the gash on her cheek was healing. She was using her bruised arm. Two stitches showed in the corner of her mouth.

"I just found out," she continued. "There's a bathtub just two doors down. Think of it. I got a bath, first one since they found Baby Joseph in the tules. Or was it Moses? I forget and forget who told me."

"Probably at a revival. Some preacher."

"Why, that's sure enough it. At a camp meeting, I remember now. I was saved." There was a glint in her one good eye.

"I washed my clothes, too, in the basin. Jesus, they was foul, after me bein' down on the floor and all."

"We'll go to the camper and gather up the rest of your clothes."

"What for? They ain't fit for a rag bag."

"One thing the sheriff wants to know, Gracie."

"I thought he knew everything."

"He's counting on you to testify against Mefford. You will, won't you?"

"What do you think I showed up with the sapphire for? Damn right I'll testify. I've stood enough from that bastard."

"Good. Now there's one thing I'd like to know."

"Shoot."

"Did you know and how did you know the sapphire would nail him?"

"Mister, I can't read nor write, but I got ears, and there's an old radio in the camper. Didn't take brains onct I seen the pin."

"Let us know if you need anything. Tell the hotel. They'll call us. See you later."

She held me up briefly, saying, "You reckon you could rustle up a nail file?"

I told her I could and went out.

Mother was hanging up sheets in the back yard. "You all right, Jase? Good. I'll be with you in a minute. Say what you will about a dryer, there's nothing like the sun to brighten up sheets." She attached the last clothespin and led the way to the house.

Inside, over coffee, I said, "I've just been to call on Gracie Jones."

"And something's on your mind?"

"More or less. She hasn't enough clothes to flag a toy bull. Just rags and few of them."

"That's demeaning to a woman."

"I rather like her."

"I'm following you, Jason. Clothes you want for her?"

"Well, yes."

"And can and will I help?"

"I know you will if you can."

"Lucky thing, Jason. For the last week or so the Ladies' Aid has been gathering castoff clothing for foreign missions or the poor or something. I donated three dresses, all with wear in them but I was tired of them, and a couple of blouses and stuff. Others donated, too."

"Any under things?"

"Of course. How big is Gracie?"

"About your size, but all angles."

"I'll comb my hair and slip on something and go see. You want to come with me?"

"I'll show up later and gather up the loot. Do you have a spare nail file?"

She didn't answer but got up, rummaged in a drawer and handed me one.

She had forgotten about lunch, though it was coming on to noon. I went to the hotel again, had something to eat and called again on Gracie. I handed her the file and asked, "What size shoes do you wear?"

She looked down at the shapeless, broken leather on her feet. "I ain't had a new pair in a coon's age and don't hardly know. Sevens, I think. What's the idea?"

"Just routine, Gracie."

I dodged in on Charleston long enough to tell him Gracie would testify. Another woman, Mrs. Innis, was on the board with Blanche.

Mother had a stack of clothing on the bedroom floor. "Quite a haul, Jason," she said. "Come help me sort it."

"We forgot about shoes."

"You mean you did. Look here."

She had picked up three pairs, all in good shape. The black ones were size 7 medium.

When we got through picking and choosing, we had two dresses, a skirt, two blouses, a pants suit and the shoes, together with under things, including a bra that Mother put in without comment. We packed all the stuff in a box.

"Gracie will bless you," I said.

"All blessings gratefully received."

So for the third time that day I knocked on Gracie's door. She opened it warily at first, without speaking, looking at the box I carried. I opened it on the bed and said, "See how these suit you."

"Me?"

"All of it you want."

She lifted a dress, saying, "Good God Almighty! I never seen the like."

She put the first dress aside and picked up a second. "If you wasn't the law, I'd think you held up a store. All clean and nice, too. Know something? I can't abide dirt. Well, blessed Jesus, here's shoes, too."

She kicked off her old ones and tried on the blacks. "They squeeze a little but that's on account of I ain't used to close fits. They're fine and dandy." Her good eye lifted to mine. "You know I ain't got a cent, but I'll pay off somehow. You know that."

"They're yours free of charge. You can thank my mother and the Ladies' Aid."

She bowed her head. "Just when you think there's no good people left, then up..." She didn't finish the sentence. She sat on the bed and cried.

I left her crying, crying over her treasures, crying because of the good people in the world.

Two afternoons later I sat with Charleston in his office. On the way in I noticed that Mrs. Stafford was on watch command. She looked composed and competent and said all was quiet.

"Isn't it supposed to be your day off?" Charleston asked me.

"I didn't take notice."

"So what's with you?"

"It's about Gracie Jones. I've been thinking."

"She's not getting difficult?"

"Not at all. But she hasn't got a cent, and neither the county nor the court is going to put out forever for room and board." I wasn't sure that was the case with a material witness. "One or the other will start yelping."

"I would think that's my concern."

"Yes, sir. Of course."

"Quit it, Jase. I'm sorry. Go ahead."

"When Susan Strand took the job with us, she left quite a few housewives in need of day help." The statement was half question.

Charleston was rolling a pencil between his fingers. "I get the drift, Jase, but I don't know."

"I want to find out more, but I know this. Gracie hates dirt. The few rags she had she kept clean. She kept that camper as neat as she could in the circumstances."

"It's a big risk. How do you know she won't steal?"

"I don't. Just a hunch."

"The language she uses would curl any good housewife's hair."

"I know. Maybe she could change, cut out the cursing."

"She might even kidnap a child."

"Never. You know that."

He put the pencil down. "The plain fact is that you like her."

"In a way, yes. I feel sorry for her."

"Talk to her some more, Jase. If you're still of your present opinion, well? It's your judgment."

"Thanks. I'll go now."

Gracie opened the door a little, then wide. I had to step back. She had on Mother's black dress, trimmed with white at throat and sleeves. She had done up her hair.

"It's me all right, Mr. Jase," she said, laughing. "Come right in."

I sat down, giving myself time for the transformation.

"It was hard with this gimpy arm, but I tried them all on. I like this one best. Don't I look grand?"

The clothes aside, she did look better. The black eye had begun to fade out. The patches were gone from her face, leaving only pink spots. The cheek gash was healing. The stitches on her mouth were still there.

"Doc Yak's been to see you," I said.

"That funny old geezer, cussin' all the time while he fixed my face. He said the stitches could come out in a couple of days. He asked me—this was for the second time—if I hadn't been drunk when I got beat up. I said again I didn't drink. Then he told me that whiskey was a friend of man, only don't get too damn friendly or it would turn against you."

"Sounds like Doc."

"I knew what he said already, but puttin' it in words kind of neats it in the mind."

"Sure. Now, Gracie, I want to sound you out. Let's both sit down. Maybe I have work for you. Just maybe."

"Kind of work I can do?"

"Day work. Cleaning house for housewives."

"I can sure as hell do that."

"Tell me the truth now. Do you have a record?"

"Record?"

"Have you ever been charged with any crime anywhere?"

"Only by you. That's a fact. Only time I ever spent in jail was your doin's. You know all about that."

"Nothing else?"

"Honest to God, Mr. Jase. Hope to die if that ain't the truth."

"In these houses there'll be temptations. There'll be some nice stuff to steal."

She drew herself up. The one eye flashed. "Well, goddamn your hide! The only thing I ever stole was that sapphire, and it was stoled already."

"Calm down. I have to make sure. Now there's your language. It's hardly fit for a nice home."

Her indignation turned into a grin. "I ain't never learned to speak proper, but I can hold back on the hells and goddamns. I can and I would."

"You want the work?"

"Damn right." She caught herself. "Yes, sir, I do."

"I'll be taking a lot on faith."

"I'd go to hell before I let you down."

"All right, Gracie. I'll see about things. Call on you later."

Susan Strand was at home. Her nose, I decided, was not so much stubborn as what my mother would call pert. She put her hand to her mouth when she saw me and asked without real alarm, "Did I do something wrong? Am I fired?"

"Nothing like that."

I told her about Gracie and her need and desire for work. I said I trusted the woman and would recommend her. "Now," I went on, "are you willing to give me the names of the people you worked for?"

She had me sit down while she wrote out a list. "Gracie's uneducated," I put in while she worked. "They may kick at her language."

She smiled, presumably at my ignorance, saying, "Not for a moment. What they want is to get the house cleaned. For that they'd put up with an army sergeant so long as he tackled the dirt."

She handed me the list. I left her and went to the office and a phone.

I had a little sales spiel made up in my mind. To each housewife I said that Gracie Jones needed work and would be available in about a week. No matter what they may have heard about her, I recommended her as good and reliable help. More, she had been highly instrumental in solving the murder of the Smitson girl, and I felt the community owed her something. How about it?

From each of them I received a firm and thankful yes.

Then I made for home, feeling like a Boy Scout, like a Boy Scout who wouldn't make Eagle rank until another murder was solved.

22

It was well after dark, and I was half-ready for bed when the telephone rang. I went to it in my bare feet, hearing the steady pound of rain on the roof. June was reminding itself that it was supposed to be our rainy month and was making up for lost time.

"Jason Beard here," I said into the telephone.

The voice identified itself. It was that of Blanche Burton. Her words came staccato. "Emergency. Meet Mr. Charleston. At the bank. Right away."

I put my shirt back on, hitched up my pants and got into socks and shoes. I hurried to the outside door, opened it and ducked back in to put on my slicker and rain hat. Not only was the rain sheeting down, but the night was dark, so black that I made my way to the car by memory, not sight.

Charleston was pulling up in front of the bank when I arrived. "Bad night. Bad business," he said, the water dripping from his oilskins.

The bank was full-lighted. Mr. Stuart met us at the door. "I told you," he said to Charleston, "I have just shot and killed a man, a brute of a man. Here is the gun." He held out, butt first, a revolver. It was probably a Colt, caliber .44 or .45, big enough, aimed right, to disable a grizzly.

About him again was that suggestion of stern control. It extended from his eyes and mouth to the trimmed beard and the three-piece suit. For a man who had just killed another, he was a study in iron reserve. He said, "Come."

We followed him, streaming, past the windows to
the rear of the bank. Roland Day sat rigid in a chair as if
transfixed. Before him on the floor lay the body of Mike
Day in a pond of blood. "There he is," Stuart said,
pointing to the body.

"You're a witness?" Charleston asked young Day
quickly as he stooped over the body.

Mr. Stuart answered for him. "Aye. He saw and
heard it all."

"We were working late," Roland put in to no
particular point. "The bank examiner comes tomorrow."
The words came from the shallows of his mind.

There was a commotion at the front door, and Doc
Yak came in, followed by Felix Underwood and two
helpers, one of whom carried a litter, the other a
covering sheet.

Doc grunted at us and knelt by the body, careful to
keep his pants out of the blood. He felt of a wrist and
stared into the open eyes. He opened Day's shirt and
examined the wound.

Over his shoulder Felix asked, "Poor devil's dead,
isn't he?"

"Oh, no, goddamnit, he's not dead. He just needs
a new heart."

Mr. Stuart said quietly, "I aimed for it."

"Killing doesn't solve anything, you damn fool,"
Doc said savagely. Death, whether from natural causes
or as a result of violence, always enraged him.

Mr. Stuart's tones still were mild, in contrast to his
words. "Fool, yourself, to speak without knowledge."

Felix said, "Can we take him?"

"Ask Charleston."

"I suppose so," Charleston said. "No need for
pictures under the circumstances. You'll have a report,
Doc?"

"Sure. I love to write themes."

The helpers lay a cloth over the body and eased it
onto the litter. The weight made them stagger a little as
they made for the door. Doc and Felix followed them,
too busy or too tired to inquire about details.

"I will give you the facts, Mr. Charleston," Mr. Stuart said.

"Not here. At the office. We'll have to detain you, Mr. Stuart."

"I came prepared." He pointed to a suitcase by the end wall. "I arranged in advance for a good woman to look after my wife."

"You came, then, determined to kill him?"

"Aye. And good riddance."

"Come along then. Both of you. In my car."

"What about mine?" Mr. Stuart asked. "There's a thing I forgot. My wife or the woman will need it."

"We'll see to that. Don't worry."

It was in character, I thought, that this dignified Scot would have an umbrella, which he opened at the door. Roland brought up the collar of his suit coat, clamped a brimmed hat on his head and ran for it. I carried the suitcase.

Blanche regarded us with interest and something of distaste as we entered the office, slopping the floor with our drips.

After we had arranged ourselves in the inner office, Charleston said, "All right, Mr. Stuart. Now for explanations if you please."

"To be sure. You must understand that in our family we regard privacy almost as one of the ten commandments, or I should say the eleventh." He looked at us for understanding as a teacher might look to make sure his point had been taken. "I would not think of opening letters addressed to my wife or of reading them unless she requested. The same is true of her. A civilized attitude, Mr. Charleston."

"Agreed."

"To proceed then," he said, again like a schoolmaster. "My daughter kept a diary. We never asked to read it and never did so secretly. Even after her death the entries seemed privileged and not for our eyes or anyone else's. We put it, unopened, with her things. Could I have a drink of water, please?"

"Something stronger?"

"No thanks. Just water."

I got it for him.

He drank and considered and went on. "Then I began to wonder about the diary. I began to think that perhaps it might bear on the brutal facts. With great reluctance I opened and read it, and it did."

"How?"

"I have the particular entry by heart. It goes: 'Last night Mr. Day offered me a ride home after practice. I had ridden with him before, and he was always all right. I better put in that he had begun calling me Pet. Then last night he stopped the car and started pawing me, making cooing noises. He tried to kiss me, or anyhow he brought his face awful close. I was scared. I squirmed away, got the car door open and ran home. I won't tell my parents, but no more Mr. Mike Day.'"

Charleston leaned forward. "That's exact? You have the diary?"

"It's exact, and I have the diary in my pocket."

"You must hand it over to us."

"And have every man jack knowing my little girl's thoughts?"

"It will not become common knowledge, I can assure you. Only what is pertinent will become known. And it will be needed as evidence, in your defense, incidentally."

With apparent misgivings Mr. Stuart handed over the book.

"So, after reading that entry?" Charleston prompted.

"I read it late this afternoon. Gradually I came to know what to do. I packed the suitcase, made the arrangements for my wife's help, and oiled the revolver. . . ."

"And came right to town, looking for Day."

"I set out after supper, thinking he would be at home then. He wasn't. I went to the bank, and there he was, in company with young Mr. Day."

"And shot him right off?"

"No. Not immediately. I cornered him and read from the diary, showing the revolver all the time. He began pleading. He said I didn't know what he had in mind for Virginia. He said I didn't know how he loved her. I knew what he had had in mind all right. I knew the kind of love he had for her. It was then, at this point, that I shot him, aiming for the heart."

"Does that statement agree with what you witnessed, Mr. Day?" Charleston asked Roland.

Roland answered woodenly. "That's the way it was. I can't repeat it word for word, but that's the way it was."

"You seem curiously unaffected by the death of your uncle."

"I'm plain struck dumb. To see a man shot and killed and him your own uncle? I don't know what to say."

Charleston's eyes went back to Mr. Stuart. "Just now, Mr. Stuart, the charge must be homicide, to be altered if at all by subsequent legal proceedings. Now I'll give you the customary warnings. . . ."

"No, please. I waive them."

"You are aware that a homicide defendant must be kept confined. He is not allowed bail or bond."

"As I have told you, I came prepared for jail. I shall plead not guilty. I do not believe that the good people of this county will ever convict me in view of the evil of my daughter's death. A father surely must be excused for avenging the abuse of his child. Call it quick justice, but justice it is."

"So be it." Charleston's gaze switched to Roland. "Mr. Day, I must ask you not to leave the county. Good night to you."

After Charleston had examined the contents of the suitcase in accordance with standard procedure, I led Mr. Stuart back to a cell.

23

After I had taken Mr. Stuart to a cell and asked
him if he wanted something from the office to read, and
he had said no, he proposed to sleep the sleep of the
just, I returned to find Charleston sitting quiet, looking
into distance. I gave him time to think, then said, "It
looks as if we have been playing catch-up all the time."
I meant to sound him out.

"Catch-up?"

"Yep. Gracie Jones solved one murder for us, Mr.
Stuart the other, and there we were, bringing up the
rear."

"Think so, do you?"

"Don't you?"

Instead of answering, he said, "I've been poaching
on your territory, Jase. Doc Yak may keep mum about
his patients, but druggists aren't so scrupulous. I know
who bought the saltpeter."

"Who was that?"

"Mike Day. He made the first purchase a couple of
weeks or so ago and another just recently."

"That muddies the water. Mike Day?"

"One explanation is that he took it to counter
senile concupiscence. There is such a thing as satyria-
sis. You are familiar with the terms?"

"You haven't lost me."

"I didn't think so. Now what is—was—your opinion of Mike Day?"

"Same as yours. He was a blowhard and a four-
flusher."

"Capable of murder?"

That was a foolish question, and he knew it. He would have answered that anybody was capable of killing, given enough provocation. But there was more in his asking than that. Now he was sounding me out. I said, "Mike Day couldn't have killed Virginia Stuart."

"Why not?"

"As if you didn't know. Because there were no drag marks from the road to that little ravine where I found her. Some indistinct footprints but no drag marks. Day couldn't have carried her that far, fleshy as he is and out of condition and getting along in years. No way."

"Exactly. Where does that leave us?"

I didn't answer. Presently he said, "Who could be so sure of the girl's virginity? Exclude her father. He wasn't in a position to know. Only examination or experience could tell for sure. I think the man spoke from knowledge. It's in your reports."

"I remember."

He looked at his watch. "Eleven-thirty. Let's go."

I knew without needing to be told that we were about to call on young Roland Day.

We put on our rain gear, went to the car, and headed for the house that Mike Day had owned. Except for a light upstairs the house was dark. The way was dark, too. I took a flashlight from the glove compartment and led on. No one answered our knocking at the front door. I tried the knob. The door was locked. We splashed around to the rear. The back door opened. It was plain then why our knocks hadn't been answered. From upstairs came the high whining and bass beat of what too many young people were calling music.

With the help of the flash we climbed upstairs. Light shone around the edges of one door. We rapped, the music stopped, and Day opened it. "What now?" he said.

"Just wrapping up loose ends," Charleston told him. "Sorry we're so wet."

"Come in then. Here." He led the way to a bathroom. "Let your things drain in the tub." I kept the flashlight in my hand, seeing no handy place to put it.

The room was ample enough, what with a rocker, two straight chairs, a chest and a bed. A good carpet covered the floor. At least it looked good from what I could see of it. The place was lighted by no more than a 40-watt bulb. Day had taken off his dark glasses. I caught the flicker of his light blue eyes. He sat down in the rocker and motioned us to the straight chairs. With his pale face, in that dim and shadowy light, he might have posed as one of the non-dead.

Seated, Charleston said, "We just thought it possible that in the absence of Mr. Stuart you could tell us something you hesitated to say in his presence. Some detail just for the sake of completion."

"I'm afraid not. His version was all right."

"Good." Charleston took a thin cigar from his pocket, lighted it and took a slow puff. "Everybody will be asking what happens to the bank now."

Day said, "I haven't had time to think about that."

"No. Of course not." He went on pursuing the subject. "Your uncle wasn't the sole owner?"

"No. A majority interest. I suppose the directors will meet."

"Forgive me, it's a highly personal question, but do you inherit?"

"If he had a will, I haven't seen it."

"But you're next of kin?"

"I guess so. That's what he told me."

"He should have known."

"I don't understand your questions. You don't think I killed him, do you?"

"No. No, indeed. A man so good to you. He gave you a good job and these quarters. I'm sure you appreciate his generosity."

"I'm grateful."

Charleston re-lit his cigar and puffed slowly like a man who had all the time in the world. Idly he asked, "Did you know your uncle was buying nitrate of potassium?"

"What's that?"

"Commonly known as saltpeter. It is used to dull and diminish the sexual drive."

Day said, "Goddamnit," at the end of a deep quick breath. "Saltpeter." He took in another lungful of air. "The old devil."

"What do you mean?"

"He said the powder would improve my complexion."

"You took it?"

"He wanted me to sprinkle it on my food, but I'm careful about what I put in my body. I said I'd take it in water, so every day in the bathroom I'd flush some down the toilet."

"You fooled him."

"I made him think I was taking it."

"I don't understand. What was his purpose?"

Day put up a hand to shade his eyes. "It's plain enough when you come to think of it. He wanted Virginia Stuart all to himself. He was crazy about her."

"And regarded you as competition? You were stuck on her, too."

"Where's the harm in that?"

"Was there any other reason for your uncle's action? Anything at all?"

"What could there be?"

"That's what I'm asking myself, but skip it for now. You were in college before you came here?"

"Yes, sir. Minnesota."

"Majoring in what?"

"Business administration."

"Did you like it?"

"Yes, sir. I was a good student."

"How far along?"

"I was about to graduate when Uncle Mike offered me the job here."

I wondered how long Day would put up with Charleston's questions. I wasn't sure where they were leading myself. The sure thing was that Charleston would persist.

"So you gave up your degree for a job?"

"Good jobs are scarce."

"I would think your uncle could have waited."

"He didn't want to."

Charleston thrust out the cigar like a pointing finger. "That's nonsense. You're lying. Why did you leave college?"

Day had shrunk back in his chair. His eyes flickered wildly. "I told you."

"Not the real reason. Speak up."

"I swear to God..."

It seemed time for me to do something besides finger the flashlight. "It's a simple matter to call Minnesota and find out. I'll phone in the morning."

Day had put both hands to his face. He was whispering, "You bastards. You dirty bastards."

"Spill it!" Charleston's command cut through the whispers.

"It was this way." Day took time for a couple of breaths. "There was a girl there I liked, and one night I tried to make up to her. I guess I tore her clothes. She screamed, and the campus police came, but it didn't amount to anything. I wasn't tried or anything like that."

"Because the girl refused to testify?"

"She knew I wasn't really serious."

"Not serious, but they kicked you out of school."

"Well, yes."

"All this explains why your uncle wanted you to take saltpeter."

"He didn't say so."

Charleston bent forward, his face grim. "If you had taken it, maybe you wouldn't have killed Virginia Stuart."

Day's voice came out weak. "Who says I killed her?"

"I do."

Now Day began sobbing. "I didn't mean to hurt her. I just wanted her, and she wouldn't have me. Can't you understand? Something came over me. I didn't mean to kill her."

"So you say. Come on. We're taking you in."

Day got up, still weeping, and went to the chest, saying, "A handkerchief." When he turned back he had an automatic in his hand. He waved it around, from Charleston to me and back. He said, "They can only hang a man once."

Charleston answered quietly, "You'll never get away with it."

"By God, I can shoot myself." The voice rose in hysteria. "Better yet, I'll kill you two first."

The gun swung toward me. I flicked the flash full in his eyes. He jerked up his gun hand against the glare. Charleston dived at him from the side. I charged his front and grabbed the hand. We went down. The automatic fired. I yanked it away. Charleston's voice came from the tumble. "Any damage, Jase?"

"None. You?"

"None."

Day had gone limp. He was mewing. We picked him up. We had no handcuffs, but I had the automatic. Charleston retrieved his cigar from the floor, and we all went down to the station and a waiting cell.

24

We were gathered again in Doc Yak's office. Present were Doc, Felix Underwood, Bob Studebaker, Charleston and I. A bottle stood on the desk, thanks to Studebaker, who would argue that I. W. Harper was as fine a bourbon as Kentucky ever distilled. With the bottle were ice and a pitcher of water.

Underwood, the last to arrive, mixed his drink, held it out, and said, "I drink to you, Chick. Hail to our sheriff."

"Better drink to Jase, here," Charleston told him. "In a pinch he's the man to have with you. I can testify to that."

Nothing would do then but that he tell about the phony grenade and the flashlight.

A light breeze came through an open window, waving the tobacco smoke in the room. The rain had ceased by early morning and, walking to the meeting, I had thought that the whole earth was breathing soft thanks for refreshment. Doc got up to flick on a light.

"All right," Underwood said, "I'll drink to you, too, Jase."

I felt uncomfortable. "Mr. Charleston overdoes it."

"I kind of feel sorry for that damn Roland Day," Studebaker said. "With a face like a whitewashed fence how was he going to get any pussy except by force?"

I answered, "I imagine Madame Simone could have fixed him up."

That kind of talk didn't please Underwood. "You talk like it was buying a pound of liver."

"Your morals are showing," Doc told him. "But I would bet that bought sex wasn't for Day. He's young and unfortunate in appearance, and he must have had dreams, dreams about the right and willing girl. Voltaire, I believe it was, said romantic love was the embroidery of the imagination woven around the stuff of nature. Day went for embroidery. That's my diagnosis."

"A sad thing all around," Felix said, for the moment forgetting the business it brought him.

"Amen," Charleston answered. "More than sad enough. But you can feel sorry for young Day if you want to. When all's said in the way of excuses and explanation, a bad actor is still a bad actor."

"Yeah," Doc jeered. "Bring on the noose. A son of a bitch remains a son of a bitch. Huh?"

"Words to that effect." Charleston sipped from his glass. "It's Mike Day you might feel sorry for."

Studebaker was quick to protest. "Why, that guy bounced a check on me, and it was to one of my distributors, and it was all the bank's fault, and then later Mike Day tried to old-pal me."

"I know." Charleston was nodding. "There were things we didn't like about him, but let's do him justice. At least give his memory credit for some decency."

"Where'd he hide it?" Underwood asked.

This time Studebaker seconded him, "And I suppose you think he didn't have an eye for that girl? He was as innocent as a lamb? No damn trace of sex?"

"Of course there was sex, but what kind of sex? Where isn't there? At least some elements of it? It affects, more or less, nearly all human behavior. Again, what kind of sex? Ask Jase here. He's studied the subject."

He turned to me, but I said, "The floor's yours."

"Not until I fix a drink." He rose, replenished his

glass and sat again. "Think on it. Some mothers find a pleasure suggestive of coitus in suckling a baby."

Underwood asked, "What's coitus?"

Doc told him, "Fucking."

"You would put it that way."

"You asked me."

"How do you know so much?" Studebaker asked Charleston. "You been interviewing milking mothers?"

"It's in reports of studies. I'm just trying to show some of the directions of sex. The father-daughter relationship is one aspect, and I'm not talking about incest. So is the father-son. The father may reject the son because he can't stand another bull in the pasture."

Doc had to add, "And the son may hate the father because the father enjoys his mother's favors."

I knew Doc would have his say. He was good at lecturing but not so good at listening.

"That all sounds like bullshit to me," Studebaker said. "Where does it take us?"

"Sorry. I've wandered all over the place, but roundabout we come to Mike Day." Charleston paused, gathering his thoughts, I supposed. Doc squirmed in his chair. The others sat waiting.

"I'll tell you two things," Charleston went on at last. "The Stuart girl kept a diary. In it she said that Day sometimes drove her home after practice, but on this last occasion he stopped the car, pawed her and brought his face close, as if to kiss her. She broke out of the automobile and ran home."

"And that proves Day's decency! For God's sake, Chick," Studebaker said.

Charleston held up a finger. "Wait. Day's last cry, before Stuart shot him, was, 'You don't know how I loved her.' He didn't say how much he loved her, just how he loved her. To my mind there's a difference."

"Now the logician speaks," Doc said.

Charleston ignored him. "Anything small, cute, innocent and vulnerable appeals to the sexual us."

"Not me," Underwood said. "No pets."

"That's why women and a good many men like to

hold babies. That's why we're attracted to puppies and kittens. We like to stroke them, to speak baby talk, to coo, even to kiss them. Mike Day was calling the Stuart girl Pet. That, I feel sure, was how he regarded her, as a pet to be babied, as a small and appealing pet. The Stuart girl wrote that he pawed her. That's wrong. In a clumsy way Mike was trying to pat her. That was natural, just as it was natural to want to kiss her cheek. That's how he loved her." Charleston repeated, "That's how he loved her."

Underwood cut in with, "You're talking against yourself. A minute ago you were throwing out explanations and excuses, and here you are excusing Mike Day."

"It's hardly the same thing, Felix. And what I think can't affect the outcome."

We were silent for a moment, then Charleston continued, "Mike wanted to protect the girl. That's why he wanted the boy to dose himself with saltpeter. He knew the boy had had trouble over a girl and been kicked out of school. And he wanted to protect the boy, too, to save him from himself. Add Mike's generosity to his nephew. He was ambitious for him and helpful to him. He couldn't believe, couldn't let himself suspect, that his nephew was guilty."

"Not with all that saltpeter in him," Studebaker interjected.

"It may be he offered the reward with some misgivings. I don't know."

Studebaker questioned him again. "What would he have done if worst came to worst and his nephew was guilty?"

"Accepted the facts. What else?"

Doc asked, "Who gets the reward?"

"With Mike dead, I doubt there'll be a reward." Charleston shook his head, and I read regret in his face. "I never thought I'd be sticking up for Mike Day, but I am. I wish I could apologize."

"Whatever the way of it was, Mike doesn't care now," Felix said.

"Lecture over, thank God?" Doc asked. "Any rebuttals? No. Then let's adjourn."

We broke up. On the sidewalk Charleston said to me, "Mike doesn't care, but I do."

"You might spare some sorrow for Mr. Stuart. I pity him."

"So do I. So do I. Private justice gone wrong again."

25

On invitation I had gone to Anita's for dinner again. We had eaten and washed up, and Omar had left us. I had brought both wine and brandy but we had hardly touched either.

I knew why I laid off. I was ready for keeps and had a proposition to make, and I didn't want to be muddled. Watching her, seeing her fresh vitality, the blooming health, the play of the day's last light on her face, I thought how beautiful she was. My opinion hadn't changed since that day when I first saw her and knew she was the girl for me. She was lovely then, and I had dated her until circumstance put us at odds. She was even lovelier now, and nothing must come between us. Not ever.

I had never been forward with girls. Reserved men, I thought, never toted up scores but surely escaped a lot of miserable regrets. I was thinking that as I looked at her. If my feeling was embroidery, then hurrah for it.

I said, "I'll be making pretty fair money in my new job."

"You've got over your doubts about the work?"

"Entirely. That was just a lapse. Call it an aberration, a passing one."

"That's good, Jase."

That subject seemed exhausted. I tried another one I had thought about. "A man wouldn't want to ask you to give up the ranch?"

"I'm really making a go of it." She added, "With Omar's help."

The shadows were gathering and she turned on a light. In any light she was beautiful.

Another subject ended until she asked abruptly, "What man?"

"Any man who put you at the top."

"Any man who loved me?"

"Sure. That's the same thing."

Her eyes met mine for a long minute. I guess they were asking me to say something more. Then she switched away and rose, and there was a note in her voice. "Don't universalize yourself."

She marched into the interior of the house. I sat, not knowing what to do. After a little while I heard her say, "Omar can take care of the damn ranch." Another moment passed. "Come here, Jase."

"I wanted to say more."

"I can't come to you. I'm not decent."

Anita in her nightgown or without it—I felt the heartbeat in my throat.

She called again. "It just came to me that you were proposing, and I just accepted. We're going to be married. Come on to bed."

I went.

ABOUT THE AUTHOR

When ALFRED BERTRAM GUTHRIE was six months old, his father moved from Bedford, Indiana, to the town of Choteau, Montana, which had a population of about two thousand. There the boy learned to know and love the high country of the West. His first experience as a newspaperman was working as printer's devil on the Choteau *Acantha*. In 1926, he went to Lexington, Kentucky, and got a job as reporter on the *Leader*, where he stayed for twenty years.

Perhaps the most important event in Mr. Guthrie's career was winning the Nieman Foundation fellowship, which took him to Harvard. There he had time to complete the writing of *The Big Sky*. In 1950, he was awarded the Pulitzer Prize for distinguished fiction.

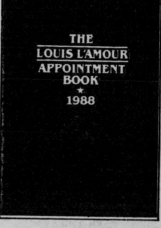

Elmore Leonard "should be a household name."
—*The Philadelphia Inquirer*

His characters become etched in your mind, his dialogue snaps off the page, and his keen understanding of the violent tensions between people who live on the edge will rivet you to your chair. Bantam offers you these exciting titles:

☐ 27099	**BOUNTY HUNTERS**	$2.95
☐ 27202	**ESCAPE FROM FIVE SHADOWS**	$2.95
☐ 26378	**GUNSIGHTS**	$2.75
☐ 26267	**GOLD COAST**	$3.50
☐ 27201	**LAW AT RANDADO**	$2.95
☐ 27097	**LAST STAND AT SABER RIVER**	$2.95
☐ 26087	**THE SWITCH**	$3.50
☐ 27098	**VALDEZ IS COMING**	$2.95

And if Western adventure is what you're after, Bantam has these tales of the frontier to offer from ELMER KELTON, one of the great Western storytellers with a special talent for capturing the fiercely independent spirit of the West:

☐ 26042	**JOE PEPPER**	$2.75
☐ 26105	**DARK THICKET**	$2.75
☐ 26147	**THE BIG BRAND**	$2.75
☐ 26449	**LONG WAY TO TEXAS**	$2.75